*A
Harlequin
Romance*

OTHER
Harlequin Romances
by ELIZABETH ASHTON

Many of these titles are available at your local bookseller,
or through the Harlequin Reader Service.

For a free catalogue listing all available Harlequin Romances,
send your name and address to:

HARLEQUIN READER SERVICE,
M.P.O. Box 707, Niagara Falls, N.Y. 14302
Canadian address: Stratford, Ontario, Canada.

or use order coupon at back of book.

MOORLAND MAGIC

by

ELIZABETH ASHTON

HARLEQUIN BOOKS

TORONTO
WINNIPEG

Original hard cover edition published in 1973
by Mills & Boon Limited.

© Elizabeth Ashton 1973

SBN 373-01741-3

Harlequin edition published December 1973

Printed in Canada

1741

CHAPTER ONE

'IF you want to spend your life looking after hordes of tiresome little brats whom nobody wants, it's your look-out, but it seems to me that you ought to have your head examined.'

Hope Castle tossed back her long strands of straight hair, and looked contemptuously at her younger sister, Charity, who had just announced her intention of training to be a nursery nurse in a children's home.

Mrs Castle, who was sitting with her two daughters, remarked pacifically:

'A nannie is quite a good thing to be. I believe there are well-paid posts to be had in families which can afford such luxuries, but is it necessary to work in an orphanage to become one?'

'They aren't called orphanages now,' Charity explained eagerly. 'They're children's homes, and there's nothing institutional about them. The children are divided into families, and each group is in charge of a house mother. The homes are graded according to ages. The one I went over the other day, and where they have a vacancy, catered for under-fives—poor little mites!'

'I daresay, but there's no need to slop over them,' Hope said severely; she had a horror of sentimentality. She was a college student, and avant-garde as her sloppy sweater, tight jeans and long, greasy hair proclaimed. Of the three Castle girls, she had the most brains and was embarked upon a brilliant career.

The eldest girl, Faith, was the beauty, and had made an advantageous marriage with the most eligible bachelor in the vicinity. Owen Foster owned an old manor house, and aped the village squire. He was stout and plain, but Faith was not romantic. His money and position more than compensated her for his lack of looks.

The Vicar of Maytree had called his three girls after the Christian virtues, and his friends believed that their names represented the saga of his desire for a son. After Faith, he had hoped, until Charity arrived and he accepted his frustration with Christian resignation.

Charity had grown up under the shadow of Faith's beauty and Hope's brilliance, and knew that she possessed neither exceptional looks or talent. She was the home bird and until her eighteenth birthday had been content to help her father and his parish, but lately he had been telling her that she ought to make something of her own life apart from her family, and the idea of working among children had occurred to her.

'I don't know why you want to go away,' Mrs Castle said fretfully. 'I know your father thinks you ought to be independent, but it isn't really necessary . . .'

'Of course it is,' Hope cut in. 'Charity can't cling on to your apron strings all her life. She needs a career, though I don't see how she's going to make one looking after someone else's kids.'

'Much better if you got married, dear,' Mrs Castle suggested, 'and had some of your own.' She wanted grandchildren, but Faith did not seem disposed to start a family, and Hope scorned matrimony. She looked affectionately at her youngest daughter's smooth brown head, around which she wore her hair in braids, her heart-shaped face and wide-spaced grey eyes. Though the rest of her features were nondescript, her eyes were beautiful.

That touched Hope off, for she was an ardent supporter of Women's Lib. Marriage was slavery, she declared. Did her mother wish to condemn Charity to the tyranny of sink and washing machine? The only bearable unions were free ones, without strings, and so on and so forth.

Charity caught her mother's eye, and smiled faintly. They had heard it all before upon Hope's infrequent visits home and both suspected it was just so much hot air. She thought it was modern and progressive to decry conventional behaviour, in the same way that she adjured respectable clothing. Her mother sometimes felt a little uneasy about her, but her father, a tolerant man, merely laughed, saying it was a phase she would outgrow, and he did not believe that she would ever practise what she preached.

'All right, Hope,' Charity said, when her sister paused for breath, 'you needn't blow your top. I've no intention of getting married. I haven't met anyone I wanted to marry, or who wanted to marry me. But I'm fond of children and I'd like to work among these poor little cast-offs, many of whom are the result of your colleagues' irresponsibility.'

'Children should be reared by the State,' Hope proclaimed.

'Even so, the State has to employ someone to change their nappies and feed them,' Charity pointed out. 'It can't be done by computers.'

That was unanswerable.

'Well, it's your life,' Hope conceded. 'But what a life!'

'It's my own choice,' Charity said equably. 'I'd hate yours.'

'Sour grapes,' Hope sneered. 'You hadn't the brains to get to college.'

'Perhaps not, but I've got a heart, which I think is more important,' Charity returned, refusing to be ruffled.

Hope duly returned to her studies and in a telephone conversation, Mrs Castle informed Faith of Charity's proposed plans. Faith took little interest in her youngest sister, and merely remarked it would do her good to get away from home before she became too impossibly parochial, but she thought she might have found something better than working in an orphanage.

'Home,' Mrs Castle said weakly.

'Same thing,' Faith retorted, and dropped the subject.

A few days later she paid the vicarage one of her occasional calls. She arrived unheralded bringing with

7

her a Mrs Dalrymple who came from the North of England, where apparently she resided in some state at a place called Carne Hall. Faith was not in the habit of bringing her smart friends to call upon her mother, and Mrs Castle was thrown into a flutter by the unexpected honour, particularly as her husband was out on parish business and was not there to support her, while Charity wondered what was behind it. Faith would not have brought Mrs Dalrymple without a motive. She was glad that she had that morning baked scones and small cakes, and she prepared tea for the visitors while her mother chatted to them. When she brought in the tea trolley, she had leisure during the pouring out ceremony to take stock of the stranger. Miranda Dalrymple was tall with aquiline features and cold greeny-grey eyes. She wore a well-cut tweed suit, brogues and a felt hat with the assured air of the born aristocrat.

While Charity handed round cups of tea and plates of food, she became aware that the cold eyes were watching her closely, and she became very conscious of her cloth skirt and woollen jumper, her usual wear, and knew that she could not be looking in the least smart. What, she wondered, did Mrs Dalrymple find interesting about her?

That, Faith soon divulged.

'Mrs Dalrymple is looking for someone to take charge of her granddaughter,' she announced. 'We thought the post might suit you, Charity. It would be preferable to going into one of those awful orphanages.'

'They're homes, not orphanages,' Charity protested, 'and they're not in the least awful, not nowadays.' Then her eyes widened as she did a double-take. 'You mean I should go to this Carne place?'

'Ours is an interesting country,' Mrs Dalrymple told her. 'Very different from this flat Essex land. Carne is on the Edge, the hills between Derbyshire and Cheshire, and I'm sure you'd enjoy a visit to it. Frances is not a difficult child, but she needs young companionship.

8

You would perhaps take her for walks, play with her and give her a few simple lessons? She has been left in my charge for a year while her parents are abroad. I'm afraid I'm a bit past entertaining small children.'

'If you're needing a sort of nursery governess,' Charity said doubtfully, 'I'm afraid I've had no experience in that direction.'

Faith moved impatiently. 'Nursery governesses are a defunct species,' she announced. 'But surely you're capable of looking after one little one? All Miranda means is you might start teaching Frances her letters. More as an amusement than anything else.'

'It's too far to take her to a nursery school,' Miranda explained, 'particularly in bad weather.'

'You wouldn't mind being isolated,' Faith seemed determined to sell this job to her sister. 'You never were one for fun and games. I'm sure you'd suit each other admirably.'

Charity was doubtful. She had not taken to Mrs Dalrymple, she seemed cold and condescending, and the idea of being alone with her and a young child in this moorland fastness was not alluring.

'I'd rather go to a home,' she insisted, 'and get a proper training. Surely you can find someone more suitable?'

Miranda said that was difficult. She had tried local girls, but they would not stay, they wanted the bright lights and complained that they could not meet their boy-friends. Had Charity got a young man?

Faith answered for her. 'Charity is not interested in boys,' she said coolly, and a gleam of interest showed in Miranda's pale eyes.

'My dear, you're quite a *rara avis* in this sex-ridden world,' she exclaimed. 'Then that will be no obstacle. Do come, I'll make it worth your while.' The cold voice was almost pleading. 'In any case it won't be for very long. You can take up your training when Martin and his wife come home. You'll be treated as one of the family. There's myself, my unmarried son—actually he's Martin's twin—and my nephew, but the men are

9

busy outside all day, so poor Frances gets left to her own devices.'

So she would not be alone with Mrs Dalrymple, but if her son and her nephew were like her, they must constitute a formidable trio. Charity began to pity the lonely little girl, but she did not want to go to far-away Derbyshire, a county about which she knew very little, except that its northern end was called The Peak.

'What do you think, Mummy?' she asked Mrs Castle.

'That it's an excellent idea,' her mother said emphatically. Already she was telling her friends in imagination, 'Charity's staying at Carne Hall with such nice people. They're County, you know.' The proffered situation was much more within her experience than working in homes. 'I think you might oblige Mrs Dalrymple,' she went on, 'since it's only for a year. Besides, you're so shy, you'll get used to being away from home, without having to mingle with hordes of strangers.'

Faith looked at her sister with a gleam in her round blue eyes.

'Don't throw away your opportunities, Char,' she said insinuatingly.

Charity could not see that Carne presented any opportunities, and she was aware of a slight aversion towards the place, which was absurd, as it was probably quite pleasant.

'I'll think about it,' she said.

Miranda looked disappointed, while Faith cried scathingly:

'Think? I thought you'd jump at it. Why on earth do you need to think?'

'I'm not leaving for several days,' Miranda said soothingly, 'so you'll have time to consider my proposition. I've some photographs of the place which you might like to see. Perhaps,' she glanced at Faith, 'you could come over to the Manor?'

Faith arranged to fetch her sister upon the following day. Then to Charity's astonishment, she asked to see her bulbs. She opened the french window that led into the garden, and her sister followed her outside.

A hedge of lilac, filling the air with fragrance, sheltered the beds of daffodils and narcissi from the east wind. They stretched between it and the house in a sheet of white and gold. Charity was proud of her flowers, but Faith had never shown any interest in them before. Nor did she now. She gave them a perfunctory glance, and drawled:

'Don't be an idiot, Char. Miranda Dalrymple has an unattached son living with her. In that lonely place you'll be thrown very much together and if you play your cards well and smarten yourself up a bit, you might manage to catch his eye. You never meet any eligible people round here, and when Miranda mentioned that she needed someone for Frances, I thought what a chance it would be for you.'

The warm blood rose in Charity's cheeks, as she exclaimed indignantly: 'Faith, how can you? I'm not looking for a husband. That's the last reason that would take me to Carne.'

'Oh, come off it!' Faith sounded impatient. 'You needn't pretend with me. Every girl's looking for a husband, it's her natural urge, whether she admits it or not. Even Hope, for all her freakish ideas, wouldn't jib at a good offer. The Dalrymples are County people, and this is your opportunity to get your feet under their table.'

Charity shrank from the vulgarity of the expression. 'I haven't your yen for important people,' she said tartly. 'They're usually snooty. As for this young man, I'm sure he wouldn't notice me, I'm not a beauty like you are.'

'I gather there won't be much competition,' Faith pointed out. 'And propinquity can work wonders. Besides, you could be quite attractive if you paid more attention to your appearance.' She looked disparagingly at Charity's skirt, which was a midi by accident, not design. 'You've a nice figure, if your clothes fitted you properly.'

11

Charity glanced at her sister's smart trouser suit, and her carefully dressed golden hair.

'I don't think Mrs Dalrymple would appreciate a nannie or whatever I'm to be in pants,' she suggested. Then lifting her chin, she added firmly, 'If I go, it'll be entirely for the sake of the child. I'm not interested in Mr Dalrymple, and I'm sure he won't be interested in me.'

Faith shrugged her elegant shoulders. 'You're hopeless!' she sighed.

Miranda's pictures of Carne showed a large square house, with curiously rounded bays on either side of a front door set above a double flight of steps. They were almost like semicircular towers, though the rectangular sash windows, three to a bay, were nineteenth-century. There were studies of trees and lawns and one photograph showing a breadth of moor. It appeared to be an impressive estate. There was no portrait of Miranda's son, but there was one of Frances, showing a fair-haired little girl, with a slightly truculent set of her mouth. This was contradicted by the expression in the child's eyes. They had a lost, almost scared look.

'That was taken to send out to her mother,' Miranda told her. 'She's rather a stupid little creature, always whining. I can't think how Martin came to beget such a moaner. All the family have been sturdy and independent.'

Charity glimpsed a Spartan hardness in this austere woman, which would make no allowances for homesickness, and Frances was not yet five. Abandoned by her parents, left to the care of this obviously unsympathetic grandmother, and no doubt an equally unsympathetic uncle, no wonder the poor mite looked lost. Charity's heart went out to her.

'If you're still of the same mind, Mrs Dalrymple, I'll be pleased to take the job,' she said impulsively. 'I ... I suppose Mr Dalrymple, your son, approves?'

'If you mean Frances' father, he left her entirely in my hands,' Miranda stated. 'As for Gabriel, it's nothing to do with him.' She smiled frostily. 'I'm hoping a young woman in the house may make him more civilised.'

Charity's eyes widened in surprise at this statement. She could hardly imagine that a son of Miranda's could be uncouth, and how could her engagement be nothing to do with him if he were, presumably, the master of Carne? But Mrs Dalrymple offered no more information and she did not like to question further.

Miranda plunged into arrangements for the journey, for she wanted to take Charity back with her, and saw no reason for delay.

Charity was a little alarmed by this precipitancy, as she realised that in an impulsive moment she had committed herself, but since she had done so, there was no point in prolonging the agony by postponing her departure. So, somewhat reluctantly, she fell in with Miranda's plans.

It was not until Faith had driven her home that she remembered that Mrs Dalrymple's nephew also lived at Carne, but since he had been dismissed with a bare mention, apparently he did not count for much in that household.

In spite of what she had said to Faith, Charity was a little curious about Gabriel Dalrymple. She had found little material in Maytree to feed her young girl's yearnings towards romance, the types that she met in the village being definitely uninspiring. At best she thought Gabriel would be shy and retiring, why else should he need 'civilising'? He might even welcome a woman friend. At worst, and which was much more probable, he would turn out to be a masculine edition of Miranda, and would look down his aquiline nose at her, ignoring her existence.

The reality was totally different from either expectation. Gabriel had come out to greet them upon their arrival and was standing above the entrance steps as the hired car which had brought them from the station drew up. It was dusk and the light behind him shone upon night-dark hair. His shadowed face was pale, the regular features clear-cut, the mouth full and sensuous. He was the handsomest man Charity had ever seen, but his was not a happy face; the beautiful dark eyes had a haunted look, the carven mouth a discontented droop. Involuntarily she thought, not the angelic Gabriel, but his colleague Lucifer after the fall.

He wore a velvet evening jacket over narrow dark trousers, with a white ruffled shirt. This costume was faintly reminiscent of the Regency period, and his appearance, combined with the old-fashioned aspect of the house, gave Charity a strange sensation of being out of period. She should have arrived by coach and worn a bonnet and shawl.

He ran down the steps as they got out of the car, and favoured Charity with a long, hard stare. Then he turned to his mother with a wry smile.

'Miss Castle—my son, Gabriel,' Miranda introduced them. 'Miss Castle's a country girl,' she added vaguely, as if this explained her lack of glamour, and in her plain tweed coat and headscarf, travel-stained and weary, Charity knew that she could not be looking at her best. Gabriel's expression had indicated that he was not impressed, and she wondered if he were disappointed by her appearance, but she had not been selected to amuse him but to look after his niece.

'Welcome to Carne,' he said hospitably. 'Though I'm afraid Carne's welcome to you will be cold. Brr ... come inside before you freeze.'

Miranda glanced apprehensively up towards the front door.

'Where's Jason?' she asked anxiously.

Gabriel shrugged his shoulders under his perfectly fitting coat. 'How should I know? Am I my cousin's keeper? He's the guardian angel, not I. He's been out all day and he hasn't come back yet.'

Miranda looked relieved and ascended the steps.

'It's as well he's out,' she said. 'It'll give Miss Castle time to settle in before he meets her.' Her tone suggested this encounter might be something of an ordeal, and Gabriel gave an impish grin. Charity realised that Jason must be the nephew. But what did Gabriel mean by calling him the guardian angel? She hoped she would not meet him tonight if he was also going to disparage her.

'Come in,' Miranda invited her. 'Don't bother about your cases, they'll be taken upstairs for you.'

Charity followed her into the hall, a vast stone-flagged space, from which a wide staircase led to the upper regions. Sporting trophies hung on the walls, stags' antlers, foxes' masks and various old-time weapons. Though it was lit by several electric lights, fitted into wall brackets resembling ancient flambeaux, the corners were full of shadow, about which there was something inimical. Again she felt as though she were moving in another age, and ought to be wearing a crinoline. Perhaps Gabriel had expected her to curtsy to him? The thought made her smile fleetingly, though in actual fact she was regretting the impulse which had brought her to this slightly sinister house among these alien people. Thinking longingly of the cosy security of the vicarage which she had left only that morning, she shivered, but not entirely with apprehension. The place was bitterly cold.

'Spring comes late to the Edge,' Miranda observed, drawing her furs more closely round her. 'Often there's still snow on the hills in March. Come into the morning room, that'll be warm.'

She led the way to one of the closed doors which were ranged round the hall. Gabriel, rather to Charity's relief, had disappeared, presumably to see about the disposal of their luggage.

The room that Miranda led her into was, as she had predicted, warm, with a huge log fire roaring in an old-fashioned grate. Heavy curtains were drawn over the window and the firelight made it look cheerful. Miranda switched on the light, and Charity saw that it was a small room, panelled in wood from floor to ceiling. There was a thick carpet on the floor and shabby but comfortable easy chairs before the fireplace. A cabinet against one wall contained an array of silver cups, and photographs of the horses which had won them, decorated the walls, with faded badges pinned to their frames, relics of past triumphs. A television set in one corner struck an incongruously modern note. The family did most of its living in that room during the winter, and early spring, the other rooms being too big to heat adequately. This Miranda explained.

'There's a drawing room, a dining room and a billiard room,' she told her. 'All huge, all arctic, but you'll find the schoolroom upstairs keeps tolerably warm and there'll be a fire in your bedroom tonight. Jason refuses to install any sort of central heating. He's Spartan, but Gabriel and I feel the cold.'

Charity moved thankfully towards the fire.

'This Mr ... er ... Jason,' she said hesitantly. 'He's your nephew?'

Miranda made a grimace, as if the subject were distasteful.

'Yes,' she said shortly. 'Jason Ollenshaw owns this mausoleum, and since he's a bachelor, he's grateful to me for running the house for him. I've been here ever since I lost my husband, and my duties include engaging the staff.'

Information that surprised Charity. Noticing that she was looking at the pictures on the wall, Miranda went on:

'Those are all champions which have won at various shows. Horses have been bred at Carne as long as there have been Ollenshaws, and that covers several hundred years. I was, of course, an Ollenshaw, before I married. Do sit down.'

She indicated a chair by the fire, and Charity sank into it gratefully, loosening her coat and taking off her headscarf.

They had dined on the train, but now an elderly woman came in asking if they needed any refreshment.

'Mrs Appleton, our housekeeper,' Miranda introduced her. 'She's been at Carne all her life. Miss Castle has come to look after Miss Frances,' she explained to the woman.

16

Mrs Appleton was stout with a weatherbeaten face from which her grey hairs were screwed back in a bun, and she wore a voluminous black dress with a cameo brooch at her throat. She looked like a being from a former century. Her shrewd dark eyes scrutinised Charity from amid a mesh of wrinkles and the girl fidgeted under her stare. Suddenly the grim face relaxed into a smile.

'Ay, lass, happen tha'll do,' she announced.

'North country people are very downright,' Miranda said with an apologetic little laugh.

'There's nowt wrong wi' that,' Mrs Appleton returned. 'Us says what us means and us means what us says.'

'Could you make us some coffee, please?' Miranda intervened.

'Reet, I'll do that. I can see you're both fair clemmed, it's cold t' neet.'

She withdrew, and Charity began to feel that she must be dreaming. The fantastic house, the handsome Gabriel and the grim old woman could not possibly be real.

'Mrs Appleton's what's called a treasure,' Miranda said drily. 'Devoted to the family, loyal, hard working and at times uncomfortably outspoken. It's a breed that's nearly extinct.'

'Have you a large staff, Mrs Dalrymple?' Charity asked anxiously. She was not used to domestics.

'Far from it. We can't get maids to stay here. Mrs Appleton does most of the cooking, I do some myself, and we have a couple living over the stables, the wife helps in the house, and Pat's the handy man. A girl from the Clough, Annie, comes in daily, and that's all. Perhaps you wouldn't mind looking after your own rooms?'

'I'd be pleased to,' Charity said, wondering how many she had been allocated.

Miranda extended long-fingered delicate-looking hands towards the fire.

'Annie waits on Frances. You and she will breakfast

in the schoolroom. Lunch we have together downstairs. Dinner . . .' She paused as Gabriel came into the room.

'I could have mine on a tray upstairs,' Charity suggested, feeling she would prefer to avoid a ceremonious meal with the family.

'Have what on a tray?' Gabriel asked. 'Dinner? Don't be absurd. Of course you'll dine with us. Do you think Carne is Thornfield Hall?'

Charity, who knew her *Jane Eyre,* laughed. The whole set-up, including her own position, did remind her of one of Charlotte Brontë's novels.

'It could be,' she said, then fearing she had sounded derogatory, added: 'I mean it has rather an old-world atmosphere.'

'It's antediluvian,' Gabriel declared. 'You'll find yourself referred to as the governess, like as not.'

'I don't mind, after all, I am something of that sort, and I'm just as plain and insignificant as Jane was.'

'Don't forget she ended up as Mrs Rochester,' Gabriel reminded her insinuatingly. 'But if you're going to fall in love with one of us, I hope it'll be me.'

He looked at her with an impudent sparkle in his eyes, and Charity blushed. Evidently he had decided to make the best of what was to hand, and was seeking a flirtation to relieve the tedium at Carne, a disquieting thought.

'That sort of thing only happens in books,' she said primly.

'Don't be so sure, even romances are often founded on fact. I don't find you plain and insignificant. You have a quaint, old-world charm, as if you were left over from the last century. Where were you brought up? In a nunnery?'

'No, a vicarage.'

'Indeed? But that's no guarantee of respectability these days. I've know some clergymen's daughters . . .' He caught his mother's warning glance. '. . . Of a different vintage altogether,' he finished airily.

Recalling Hope's avant-garde aspirations and Faith's mercenariness, Charity smiled; they were very different from herself.

'Being the youngest of three girls, I've been rather sat upon,' she admitted frankly.

'And now you've flown from the nest, you're itching to try your wings?' he suggested. 'You must let me assist you with your first flutterings.'

She did not know quite what to make of this remark, and threw an appealing glance towards Miranda, who had been watching them indulgently. Mrs Dalrymple came to the rescue by reverting to the question that had been under discussion when Gabriel came in.

'Regarding dinner, you can do as you please,' she said.

'Then I'd sooner stay upstairs,' Charity decided. She had no evening dresses. 'If that's convenient.'

Gabriel looked at her in mock despair.

'That's too bad of you,' he declared. 'I was looking forward to having someone young at the dinner table. We only call it dinner out of deference to my mother's prejudices, but actually it's only supper. Why do you want to deprive us of your company? Do you find us objectionable or do we overawe you?'

'Well, I do feel a little overawed,' she confessed shyly.

Gabriel sat down, drawing up a chair beside her, and her heart quickened at his proximity. It was the first time in her life that she had been so close to a fascinating male.

'You needn't be,' he assured her. 'We may seem to live in the dark ages, but we don't bite, though Jason is a bit grim and forbidding. For your information ...' he shot her an ambiguous look, 'he's completely insulated against the charms of your delightful sex.'

'That's no concern of mine,' Charity told him with heightened colour. Gabriel's mind seemed to run along the same track as Faith's did.

'You're in an advantageous position,' Gabriel drawled. 'A maid among unattached males.'

'Oh, please ...!' Charity protested, and again glan-

19

ced appealingly at the apparently indifferent Miranda, and then to her relief Mrs Appleton brought the coffee in. Gabriel sprang up to place a small table in front of Miranda to accommodate the tray.

'Will that be all, ma'am?' the old woman asked.

'Yes, thank you. Goodnight.'

The housekeeper withdrew and Gabriel remarked:

'There's another relic for you. I don't suppose you've ever seen anyone like Mrs Appleton before still in harness.'

'We'd be in a bad way without her,' Miranda rebuked him, and proceeded to pour the coffee. Charity noticed that the pot was silver and the cups Crown Derby. Gabriel passed one to her and as she took it, their fingers touched. A little thrill ran along her nerves at the contact.

'Thank you, Mr Dalrymple,' she said demurely.

'Oh no!' he exclaimed. 'You must call me Gabriel. What's your name? I refuse to "Miss Castle" you.'

Charity thought Mrs Dalrymple would disapprove of this informality, but to her surprise, Miranda smiled and said:

'Her name is Charity.'

'I don't think you ought to use it,' Charity objected. 'I'm not a guest here, I've come to look after Frances.'

'I don't see why you shouldn't use your first names,' Miranda declared. 'After all, this is a democratic age.'

'Carne's still feudal,' Gabriel said sourly. Then he smiled. 'By your leave, I shall call you Charity.'

Charity had an uneasy feeling that the use of her first name might make it more difficult to keep Gabriel in his place, which looked like being necessary. She glanced again at Miranda. Her complacency was a little puzzling; she seemed to be deliberately encouraging intimacy between the two of them.

'On second thoughts I think Charity will have to come down to dinner,' that lady remarked. 'We can't expect Annie to keep running upstairs with trays.'

Charity flushed. 'But don't you ... dress?' she faltered.

20

'Not really. We change, as we wear sports clothes all day, but not into anything elaborate. Haven't you got a thin frock that would do?'

'Have a heart, Ma!' Gabriel exclaimed. 'The dining room's like the North Pole.'

'I expect she's got a wrap of some sort,' Miranda said vaguely. She stood up. 'If you're ready, Charity, I'll show you your room.'

'But you'll come down again?' Gabriel asked eagerly.

Charity said no, it was late and she wanted to unpack.

'Oh well, there's always tomorrow,' he said easily, and went to open the door for them.

Charity had been allocated practically a whole suite of rooms. The so-called schoolroom was a comfortably furnished sitting room, with a deal table set before the window to justify its name.

'Frances makes such a mess with her ploys,' Miranda seemed to be actually apologising for its presence. A fire was burning although the room was empty. 'It soon gets chilly if it goes out,' she explained. 'We've plenty of fuel. Jason gets a truckload from the pithead every winter and there's a lot of wood on the estate.'

A door led out of the schoolroom into Charity's bedroom, in which another fire had been lit. A second door connected it with Frances' room, and they had their own bathroom.

'It's all lovely,' Charity said appreciatively.

'Then if you've got all you want, I'll say goodnight.'

Charity glanced towards the closed door. 'Could I see Frances?' she asked, for the child was the reason for her presence. 'That is, if I won't disturb her, of course.'

'Certainly, if you wish.' Miranda sounded faintly surprised. 'She'll be sound asleep.'

She opened the door to disclose the wan flicker of an old-fashioned nightlight. The room was small and was furnished in white wickerwork. It was strewn with dolls and toys, mingling with items from the child's wardrobe.

'Annie seems incapable of making the child tidy,' Miranda said, looking round her distastefully. 'I hope you'll be more successful.'

She moved to the narrow bed and stood looking down at its occupant, and Charity joined her.

Frances Dalrymple lay in a huddle clutching a teddy bear, her fair tousled hair spraying the pillow. In the dim light, Charity could only glimpse a flushed pink cheek and a dark crescent of lashes covering one eye. The child muttered something and snuggled further into the bedclothes.

Miranda tried to remove the teddy bear, but even in her sleep, Frances' hold would not relax.

'An unhealthy habit,' Miranda whispered to Charity. 'But she won't go to bed without it. Refuses to go to sleep unless she's cuddling it.'

Charity said nothing, but she suspected that the toy represented solace for a deprivation, probably of affection. She glanced at the still, pale face of her employer which expressed nothing except a slight impatience. Grandmothers were supposed to be indulgent to their grandchildren, but not this one. She was hard as nails. Any maternal softness she might have once possessed seemed to have frozen.

When they withdrew, Charity left Frances' door slightly ajar. The child had seemed so terribly alone shut in her room.

Having bestowed her clothes in the large Victorian wardrobe and chest of drawers, Charity undressed in luxury in front of the fire. Then she discovered that she had left her handbag downstairs. It was not an article she wanted to mislay, as not only did it contain her money, but also her diary and several letters with comments not intended for prying eyes. Reluctantly she decided that she must retrieve it.

She put on her dressing gown and hoped fervently that she would not encounter anyone upon her journey to the morning room. The house seemed deserted, and when she tapped upon the door, there was no response. Cautiously she pushed it ajar and was pleased to discover it was empty and unlit except for the glow from the dying fire. Her bag was by the chair which she had occupied, and picking it up, she turned to retrace her steps.

'Who the deuce are you?'

She started violently. The voice, sharp and peremptory, seemed to come out of nowhere. Then she realised that a shadowy figure was standing in the doorway, barring her retreat. Since she did not recognise it, it must belong to someone whom she had not yet encountered, and her heart sank. She had met enough strangers for one evening.

Whoever it was reached out an arm and switched on the light, bathing the room in a sudden glare. Defensively Charity clutched her bag to her breast, and blinking stared at the newcomer.

It was a man dressed in riding clothes, jacket, yellow pullover, breeches and boots. He was not much over medium height and so slim that a casual glance would never suspect his wiry strength, for though he was on the wrong side of thirty, there was not a spare ounce of flesh on his muscular body. His face was lean and brown, distinguished by a slightly aquiline nose, his only resemblance to Miranda, and his fine short hair was the same colour as his skin. He reminded Charity of a racing greyhound; he had the same appearance of high breeding and abounding energy. The piercing eyes that regarded her from under knitted brows were startlingly blue.

'I ... I'm Charity Castle,' she stammered.

'Indeed?' He raised eyebrows that were indistinguishable from the colour of hair and complexion. 'What, may I ask, is Charity Castle doing at Carne?'

'I ... I'm the new nurse ... to look after Frances.'

He ripped out an oath and strode to her side. He took her shoulders in a steely grip and turned her so that the light fell full upon her face. The keen blue eyes appraised her from her loosely flowing brown locks to her slippered feet, noticing her extreme youth and the anxious appeal in her big grey eyes. The quilted dressing gown was unrevealing, but it was an unconventional garb for a nannie.

'You're telling me that my aunt, Mrs Dalrymple, has engaged you, *you*, to look after Frances?' There was a rasp in his voice.

She nodded, too overcome to speak.

'She should have had more sense!' he exclaimed angrily, releasing her shoulders, which she was sure would show bruises. 'You're only a child yourself.'

'I'm nearly nineteen,' she returned with an attempt at dignity. 'And though I'm inexperienced, I'm sure I'm capable of managing one small girl.' Her face softened to tenderness as she recalled the image of Frances cuddling her teddy bear. 'But I think she needs love and sympathy more than managing,' she added.

Her questioner noticed the beauty of her eyes and the gloss on her long, fine hair, which half veiled her face, and his frown returned.

'I don't doubt you can cope with ... Frances,' he told her, the pause before the child's name conveying that there were other problems less easy of solution. 'Is it a habit of yours to run round the house in a state of undress?'

The way he spoke and was eyeing her was an insult and she flushed miserably.

'I ... I know it must seem odd,' she stammered, 'but when I was ready for bed I found I'd forgotten my handbag. I ... I hoped I wouldn't meet anyone ...' She held the bag out towards him as testimony of the truth of her words.

'It would have been better if you'd dressed yourself before coming down,' he said shortly. 'When did you arrive?'

'This evening,' she faltered, looking at him uncertainly. If this were the cousin, the Jason Ollenshaw who owned Carne, it was important that she should give him a good impression of her, but she had been caught at a disadvantage, literally with her hair down, seeming more like an irresponsible schoolgirl than a sedate nursery nurse. Endeavouring to appear dignified, she

24

said formally:

'I suppose you're Mr Ollenshaw?'

'So you *have* heard of me.' He was sarcastic. 'I wondered whether my good aunt had mentioned my existence. Yes, I'm Jason Ollenshaw, and I've only just got home, so I missed your arrival, but I suppose my cousin was there to greet you?'

His eyes narrowed as he put the question.

'Yes, I've met Gabriel ... I ... I mean Mr Dalrymple.' She crimsoned at the slip. She did not think Jason would approve of the familiarity of first names, and as his face sharpened suspiciously, she knew that she was right.

'So,' he said, 'you've met Gabriel.' He emphasised the name. 'And I see he's wasted no time.'

'I'm sorry,' she murmured confusedly. 'I ... I didn't mean to sound ... I mean, hearing Mrs Dalrymple call him that ... really, I do know my place.'

'Do you? I hope so.' A mocking gleam came into his eyes. 'Sit down, Miss ... what did you say your name was?'

'Castle, Charity Castle.'

'A pretty name,' he said surprisingly. 'Well, Miss Castle, I've something to say to you.'

'Won't it keep? I'm awfully tired,' she protested.

'I won't keep you long,' he said more gently, and repeated, 'Sit down.'

It was a command. Obediently she subsided into her former seat and pulled her gown as far as it would go over her bare legs.

He went to a cupboard in the wall, which he unlocked and took out a bottle and a couple of cut-glass wine glasses, which he proceeded to fill.

'This will revive you,' he said, bringing one to her. She took the glass of amber liquid doubtfully, while she noticed that he was careful to relock the cupboard after replacing the bottle, putting the key on the ring he pocketed. A distrustful sort of man, she thought, locking up his drinks and regarding her with suspicion.

'All the best,' he said absently, holding up his glass. He sat down on the chair opposite to her and again subjected her to that close, disapproving scrutiny. Embarrassed, she asked tentatively:

'Didn't you know I was coming?' for it seemed unlikely Miranda would have engaged her without his knowledge.

He smiled, a charming smile that lit up his rather stern face.

'I knew someone was coming,' he told her, 'but I was given to understand she was a Vicar's daughter, a desiccated spinster of uncertain years whom Mrs Dalrymple picked up during her visit to Essex, so you see your appearance gave me a shock, and I must apologise for my bad manners. I was not expecting to meet a pretty young girl running about in her negligée.'

'I've explained about that,' she said stiffly, 'and I'm not pretty. My eldest sister Faith's the pretty one, and Hope's clever. I'm just nondescript Charity.' Nervousness made her garrulous, giving him information that could not possibly interest him.

'With such names you could only be a vicar's daughters,' he announced amiably, 'but that's your only qualification for this post.' He paused, and added with a gleam in his eye, 'And I wouldn't call you nondescript.'

'Oh, but I am,' she insisted, 'and as regards Frances, I'll do my best to give satisfaction.'

'I don't doubt it,' his tone was dry, 'but your best mayn't be ... adequate. Deuce take it!' He stood up, putting his glass on the mantelpiece. 'I won't hedge, Miss Castle. Carne is no place for a young girl, it's too lonely, you'll only get into mischief. Tomorrow I'll put you on the train back to London.'

'Oh no, please,' she cried out in consternation. 'I ... I'm used to being alone. Won't you please at least give me a trial?'

He took her glass from her, eyeing her with the intentness of a hawk.

'You seem very anxious to stay,' he observed. 'I

26

should have thought the first sight of the place would have put you off, but you've also seen Gabriel; is that why you want to stay so badly?'

He shot the question at her, as if he hoped to trip her into an admission, but the blank stare she gave him was uncomprehending.

'But Mr Dalrymple's nothing to do with me,' she said, bewildered. 'I want to stay because I've seen Frances, and it seems to me ...' She stopped. It was hardly her place to criticise his aunt to him.

'Well?' he queried. 'What seems to you?'

'I may be quite wrong,' Charity went on carefully, 'but I've a feeling no one really wants her here, and I was drawn to her at once, poor little thing. I'm sure I could help her. Do let me try.'

The man's hard, leathery face softened unexpectedly. 'Poor little Fran,' he said gently. 'My aunt has no use for girls. If Fran had been a tomboy, she might have got by, but she's timid and Miranda has only contempt for her.' He looked searchingly into Charity's wide, beseeching eyes. 'I don't want to deprive her of your services,' the dryness was creeping back into his voice, 'which no doubt would benefit her, but you're too great a responsibility—you see, there are other considerations.'

'Such as?'

He was filling his pipe, standing with one foot on the fender, the firelight reflected in his shining boot. There was a dapper spruceness about his whole appearance that Charity was unwillingly finding exceedingly attractive. He had not Gabriel's melancholy handsomeness, but there was something clean and clear-cut about him, suggesting the outdoor life he led. He looked absurdly young, for she knew he must be considerably older than herself, but he had that ageless look which belongs to a certain type of lean, horsey men, who change little with the passing years. He took his time about answering her query, lighting his pipe with a match and bending to throw the stalk into the fire, then straightening himself, he looked at her, the very blue eyes keen as a knife blade.

'Frankly, I don't want any complications with Gabriel,' he said bluntly.

A wave of burning colour swept over her face, as she cried indignantly:

'But that's absurd! Mr Dalrymple doesn't come into my province.'

'He may invade it,' Jason was dry. 'My cousin is susceptible, and not only are you very young, but you can't have learned much about life and men in your vicarage.'

'Oh, haven't I,' she returned with a flash of humour. 'You'd be surprised at what goes on in a country parish.'

'I've a good idea,' he told her. 'This also is a country parish, but Gabriel ...' His face darkened. '... No, I can't risk it.'

Her heart sank. 'I know I must appear to be terribly unsophisticated,' she said hesitantly, 'but I'm not ignorant of ... those sort of risks.' He raised his brows quizzically. 'You see, I've got a sister who's a hippy.' She was maligning Hope, but somehow she must persuade this dour man that she could cope with his cousin. 'She's told me all about the permissive society.'

'Has she indeed?' Jason with difficulty suppressed his amusement. 'I don't allow any permissiveness at Carne,' he added with mock severity. His eyes came to rest upon her bare ankles.

Charity felt she had blundered. 'I don't hold with it myself,' she said hastily, 'and I'll be ever so discreet.'

'Will you?' his mouth twitched. 'Unfortunately I've no great opinion of the discretion of the modern miss.'

He turned his gaze to the fire, and she waited, twisting her hands together, not knowing what to say next. Involuntarily her eyes went to the knife-sharp profile presented to her, and she noticed how exceedingly well shaped was the smooth brown head, and how proudly it was set upon his square shoulders, the slightly arrogant curve of his haughty nostrils, above the close-lipped mouth and strong chin. A dangerous man to thwart, she thought with a shiver of apprehension, but a very masculine man, a mature man; he made Gabriel seem like a pretty boy. At length he turned his head and she dropped her eyes, unable to meet that penetrating, quizzical gaze.

'If I let you stay, you must promise me not to make any assignments with Gabriel.'

'But of course, such a thing would never occur to me,' she assured him, her hopes rising.

'Wouldn't it? Even though he's undoubtedly good-looking, and of course you know that if I don't marry, and I've no intention of doing so, he'll inherit Carne? Quite a good match for an enterprising young woman.'

Uncomfortably she remembered that Faith had made practically the same observation, and her colour rose.

'Isn't it very unlikely that Mr Dalrymple will want to date me?' she suggested, 'and if he should show such bad taste, I promise faithfully I won't encourage him.'

'Do you keep your promises?' he asked doubtfully.

That was too much! She sprang to her feet, her eyes dark with anger.

'Mr Ollenshaw, what do you think I am?' she cried vehemently. 'I've come here to look after a child, not to find a husband, or a lover. Frances is my only concern and I'm not the least interested in Mr Dalrymple or his prospects, nor yours either.'

'The lady protests too much, methinks,' he quoted drily. 'You've made out a good case for yourself, but I still find it a little difficult to believe that any young girl could be willing to bury herself at Carne without an ulterior motive. No doubt my aunt explained the—er—layout to you when she engaged you?'

'Yes,' she admitted, unwillingly again terribly conscious of Faith's remarks about Miranda's unattached son, 'but I was only interested in Frances, she didn't say much about anybody else, and now I've come, I won't abandon that poor little girl because of your ridiculous suspicions.'

'All right, relax,' the thin-lipped mouth twisted

humorously. 'But I can make you go, you know. I'm master here, whoever my aunt takes upon herself to engage.'

'Mrs Dalrymple thought I was suitable,' Charity said defensively. 'I didn't want to come until I saw a photo of Frances. She looked so pathetic.'

'So you're sentimental about children,' he observed a little scornfully, and she reflected that he was as hard and austere as Miranda. No wonder Frances looked pathetic! The anger died out of her as she thought of the child.

'Please let me stay,' she said quietly, 'for Frances' sake.'

He seemed to be again considering her, while a brooding silence filled the room. Charity shifted uneasily under the unblinking stare that he fixed upon her, as if he would penetrate to her very soul. The man regarding her was quite insufferable in his pride and arrogance. He wanted to send her away on the mere possibility that she might become entangled with his heir. She was not good enough to mate with the future master of Carne and that was the reason for his reluctance to tolerate her presence in his home. The propinquity Faith had counted upon was the danger that he wanted to avert, for she could not imagine her charms were sufficient to attract Gabriel without the spur of loneliness. Pride urged her to fall in with his wishes, to leave Carne next day and never see this objectionable man again, but the recollection of a flushed baby face, the pathos of small hands clutching a teddy bear restrained her, she would not allow Jason such an easy victory. She was more than ever convinced that her presence was necessary to stand as a bulwark between the child and her hard and unfeeling relatives. If Jason was adamant, she would appeal to Mrs Dalrymple, persuade her to plead for her and testify to her character.

The sound of a log falling in the grate made her start, and she lifted her small determined chin and stared disdainfully back at the master of Carne.

'I'm sorry you seem to think I'm a sort of adventuress,' she said coldly, 'but actually I wouldn't know how to set about catching a man, and if I give you my word, and I do keep my promises, that I won't have anything to do with Mr Dalrymple beyond common courtesy, will that satisfy you?'

He was still eyeing her doubtfully, then his face creased to a smile, and the tension broke.

'Very well, I agree to give you a trial,' he conceded, 'though it goes against my better judgment.'

'If you can't trust me ...' she began heatedly, and he held up his hand to check her.

'Where women's emotions are concerned they can't be trusted,' he said contemptuously. 'Don't let yours become involved, that's all.'

'Do you know so much about women?' she asked daringly, provoked by his obvious scorn for her sex.

'Though I'm an old bachelor, I'm not without experience,' he retorted, and she wondered where he had obtained it. 'And I assure you I'm quick to notice signs and portents. If I discover any hanky-panky between you and Gabriel, back you go on the next train. Goodnight, Miss Castle.'

The dismissal was so abrupt, she stood hesitating, hardly able to believe that she had won her point.

'Goodnight, Mr Ollenshaw,' she said at length, and turned to the door.

'One moment, you've again forgotten your bag.' He was holding it out to her, his eyes again suspicious. As she went to take it, she wondered if he dared to imagine she had left it behind on purpose.

'Thank you,' she murmured.

'And in future don't come downstairs undressed,' he cautioned her. 'Your great experience of men,' he was laughing at her now, 'should have warned you that such apparel puts ideas into male minds.'

The idea it had put into his mind, that she had come down thus clad hoping to meet his cousin, was unjust and unfounded, but it still seemed to be lingering, in spite of all her denials.

'Perhaps you'd like me to go about in my overcoat,' she cried, her eyes sparkling irefully.

'That'll hardly be necessary, unless you're cold,' he returned gravely, deliberately misunderstanding her. 'There have been winters when my aunt has worn furs at the dinner table, but luckily for you the summer is coming.' Rather to her surprise he opened the door for her. 'Goodnight again, Miss Castle.'

She went out, passing him with lowered eyes and heightened colour, and ran upstairs, filled with passionate resentment. Never before in her whole life had she met such a hateful man as Jason Ollenshaw!

As Charity climbed into bed, it occurred to her that there was one feature of the situation that definitely did not tally. Jason's attitude was understandable, if humiliating, but Miranda Dalrymple, that proud aristocrat, had been insistent upon her engagement, though she must have foreseen the possible consequences. Moreover, during the evening she had deliberately encouraged Gabriel's advances towards herself, and she had been so keen to bring Charity to Carne that she had misled her nephew regarding her age and appearance. It seemed almost as if she wanted to bring about the complications that Jason feared. Why? Her attitude was definitely puzzling and Charity could find no key to it. She was still cogitating upon it when she fell asleep.

CHAPTER TWO

CHARITY awoke to find the sun was shining through the chinks in the window curtains. She looked at her clock and saw it was seven o'clock, and breakfast, she had been told, would not appear until eight-thirty. She sprang out of bed, pulling on her dressing gown and ran to the window, drawing back the curtains and pulling up the sash to enable her to lean out and view her surroundings, oblivious of the early morning chill.

She discovered that her room was at the side of the house. Directly below her was a gravel path, beyond which was a terraced lawn, levelled out of the slope of the hill upon which the hall stood. It terminated in a large flower bed and a very high wall.

To her right was a shubbery containing rhododendron bushes, just beginning to show colour, backed by tall trees. A wing of the house went out to meet it, so that the garden was enclosed upon three sides.

She leaned further out, looking to her left, for there the flat lawn ended in a steep bank dropping to a low wall, beyond which a green field descended to the Clough Bottom, where a gleam of water showed among trees. On the further side of the valley, the ground rose sharply to the bare slopes of a conical hill, which dominated the landscape.

The field below the garden was bisected by a stone wall, and her quick ears caught the sound of thudding hooves. Then, as she watched, a horse and rider appeared, the horse taking the wall in a splendid arc of a leap. Safely landed, the rider reined in and Charity recognised her interrogator of the night before, Jason Ollenshaw, the master of Carne.

The sun shone on the horse's gleaming chestnut coat, the creamy fall of mane and tail. Walking now, shaking his head against the restraining bit, the beast moved with the springy step of a thoroughbred, a creature all fire and high spirit, the man upon his back looking like part of him.

Jason appeared at his best on horseback, and he too looked like a thoroughbred; he had the same clean lines as the horse. Both suggested leashed power, that of the animal controlled by the man, the man by his indomitable will.

Charity drew back hastily, though it was unlikely that Jason would notice her and he was already passing from view. She shut the window, realising that she was cold, and made a leisurely toilet. Then she went into Frances' room.

The little girl was awake and sitting up in bed, still hugging her teddy bear. As Charity came in and went to draw the curtains, she followed her movements with anxious blue eyes, eyes as blue as her cousin Jason's. Frances was a true Ollenshaw, having inherited nothing from the darker Dalrymple strain, which was manifest in her Uncle Gabriel.

'Good morning, Frances.' Charity said cheerfully.

'Goo' morning.' The child spoke doubtfully. 'Is you my new nannie?'

Charity sat down at the foot of the narrow bed.

'Yes,' she affirmed. 'I hope you and I are going to be great friends.'

She smiled reassuringly at the child, but Frances did not respond. Instead she shrank back on her pillow, her eyes wide with apprehension.

'You won't smack me?' she whispered.

'Good gracious, no!' Charity exclaimed, surprised.

'Even when I'm bad?'

'No.' Charity was emphatic. 'I don't believe in smacking children. Whoever put such an idea into your head?'

'Uncle Gabby.' The child's lips were trembling. 'He said you'd shut me up in the dark and give me only bread and water.'

'Your uncle was only teasing you,' Charity told her, suppressing a hot wave of indignation at this misplaced humour. The unfortunate child had taken his

34

remarks seriously.

Anxious to dispel the image of a stern monitor, which Gabriel had tried to instil, she went on coaxingly:

'You and I are going to have fun together, and you mustn't be afraid of me. I wouldn't hurt you for the world. Now, aren't you going to get up?'

Frances did not move, and continued to eye her new attendant suspiciously and in silence.

'What are you going to put on?' Charity asked.

'My jods,' Frances said tonelessly.

'Your what?'

Frances indicated a pile of clothing on a chair. 'It's my riding lesson after breakfast,' she explained.

'Oh, I see.' Enlightened, Charity picked up the miniature pair of jodhpurs. 'How nice,' she went on. 'Do you like riding?'

'I hate it, it's horrid,' Frances burst out, her eyes filling with tears. 'My gran says I got to.'

Not knowing quite what to say, Charity murmured inadequately:

'I expect you'll get to like it in time.'

She wondered if Mrs Dalrymple was aware of her granddaughter's aversion to that form of recreation. It did not seem right to her that the child should be forced into a pursuit which she disliked, and quite possibly frightened her.

Frances tightened her childish lips in an expression which conveyed that never in a hundred years would she permit herself to enjoy riding.

Charity assisted with Frances' reluctant ablutions, which the child considered unnecessary, since, as she pointed out, she had a bath every night.

'But you must sponge your face to freshen yourself,' Charity insisted.

'Don't want to be fresh,' Frances declared, wriggling.

Eventually she was got into her clothes and her hair brushed and combed with something of a struggle. Frances disliked the comb even more than the sponge. She looked frail, but she had a will of iron and Charity

35

realised her task was not going to be all sweetness and light.

Annie brought in their breakfast. Frances ate a few mouthfuls of egg, and drank half a cup of milk, but refused anything else, saying she was not hungry.

'But you won't grow into a big strong girl if you don't eat,' Charity told her.

'I will,' Frances contradicted her, 'and when I'm a big girl, I won't ever eat egg, and I won't ever go riding and I won't have a nasty, horrid old nannie,' she concluded triumphantly, with a sly look at Charity's carefully schooled face. Charity decided to let this assertion pass, and smiled a little wryly as she recalled how she had pleaded with Jason Ollenshaw for the care of this child. It was not going to be easy to win Frances Dalrymple's love and confidence.

Miranda came in as they were finishing their meal, and instantly Frances shrank into herself. She whispered, 'Goo' morning, Gran,' but her eyes were wary.

'Getting to know each other?' Miranda said brightly, and Frances scowled. Her grandmother paid her no further attention, but proceeded to outline the day's routine for Charity. The riding lessons were a daily occurrence when it was not actually pouring with rain. 'Both families are born horsemen and horsewomen,' Mrs Dalrymple stated proudly. 'I used to hunt myself, but Martin doesn't keep a stable now, so this is an opportunity for Frances to learn.'

'Isn't she a little young?' Charity hazarded, knowing Frances' sentiments.

'Not at all. I rode almost before I could walk,' Miranda informed her.

She went on to say that after the riding, perhaps Charity would give her charge some simple lessons. They would come down for lunch, and in the afternoon go for a walk whenever it was fine.

'Frances has been cosseted too much,' she said. 'I want her to grow sturdy in our fine air. We have a saying, "Derbyshire born and Derbyshire bred, strong in th' arm and wick in th' head." Wick being an old word meaning quick, not weak, as our decriers like to make out. Of course Carne is really over the border, but we always think of it as Derbyshire.'

When she had gone, Frances asked, 'What's cosseted?'

'Being fussed over,' Charity explained.

'I likes being fussed,' the child said wistfully.

Charity had seen children not much older than Frances riding confidently at local gymkhanas. They rode small, quiet and sometimes definitely fat ponies. She was quite unprepared for the mount provided for Frances. They had gone out of the side door of the house, up some steps, and through an archway into a stone paved yard at the back of the Hall. There the man Pat awaited them, holding a bay mare and a frisky pony. The latter was all of twelve hands, and looked full of spirit, tossing his head and rolling the whites of his eyes. Attached to his bridle was a long leading rein.

Gabriel Dalrymple came to join them, wearing riding kit. He looked even more handsome by daylight, and he smiled at Charity before turning to his small niece.

'Well, Fran, feel up to jumping a five-barred gate?' he asked facetiously. 'Your gran wants you to ride with me this morning instead of plodding round the field on old Dobbin.'

Frances shrank against Charity, and she realised that the child was terrified of the skittish pony.

'Isn't that beast rather too lively for a beginner?' she asked anxiously, 'and surely you don't expect her to ride beside you on that big horse?'

'Oh, she'll stick on somehow,' he said casually. 'You don't think I'm going to run beside her, do you? She'll have to take a toss or two before she's a horsewoman.'

Frances was shaking with terror.

'Mr Dalrymple, I won't consent to this,' Charity declared firmly. 'It's sheer cruelty!'

His eyebrows went up. 'Do you ride?' he asked suavely.

'A little.' Her experience consisted of childish exploits with the vicarage pony.

'Here we're all experts,' he boasted, 'and my mother is set upon Frances becoming proficient.'

'You're going the wrong way about it,' she insisted. 'To perform any sport well, the first essential is confidence. Frances will never acquire that if you terrorise her.'

For a second a devil seemed to look at her out of his black eyes. Then he laughed.

'My dear Charity,' he said, and the way he spoke her name sounded like a caress, 'you know nothing about it. Your province is the nursery, the stable is mine. Come . . .' he held out his hand to Frances.

The child looked up at him piteously.

'I don't want to tumble,' she cried.

'The ground's soft enough,' Gabriel told her callously, 'once we've got out of the yard, and surely you can stick on that long. Come on, up with you.'

Frances clung desperately to Charity's skirt. 'No!' she shrieked. 'No, no!'

Gabriel wrenched her roughly away and carried her towards the pony, which, alarmed by Frances' cries, had begun to dance. Pat tried to remonstrate with Gabriel as he sought to quieten the two nervous animals, but Gabriel paid him no heed. Charity looked wildly round, wondering to whom she could appeal. If Gabriel had his way she foresaw a nasty accident.

Then Jason walked into the yard. In one swift glance he took in the situation.

'What's going on here?' he asked. He had not raised his voice, but instantly everyone, even the restive horses, became still. Gabriel had succeeded in dumping Frances upon the pony's back, and she was clinging to the pommel of the saddle, tears pouring down her cheeks.

'Mr Ollenshaw,' Charity cried, 'please stop them!'

He disregarded her; his eyes were upon Gabriel who was slashing his boot with his riding crop and looking sullen.

38

'Take that child off Mischief at once,' he commanded.

Gabriel did not move; it was Charity who ran forward and lifted Frances down, clasping her protectively in her arms.

'My orders were that Frances was to be mounted on old Dobbin,' Jason went on. 'Mischief is unsuitable for an infant. You might have killed your niece.' The steely eyes were fixed accusingly upon his cousin.

Gabriel smiled impudently. 'You're exaggerating, old man,' he drawled. 'Mother's been getting at me, saying Fran wasn't improving. She said she never would ambling along on Dobbin, so I thought we'd try something more ambitious. Mischief couldn't bolt on a leading rein.'

'He's been known to buck,' Jason said shortly. 'Truth is you've no patience with the kid and her old pony, but to put her up on Mischief, who's only half broken, was a sheer act of lunacy—or worse.'

'I didn't realise Mischief's education hadn't been completed,' Gabriel returned. 'You've been trying to sell him to the Moorside Pony Club, so if it isn't, aren't you being guilty of sharp practice?'

Jason did not deign to answer this thrust; instead he said coldly, 'If you're going for a ride, you'd better be off.' He walked towards Charity. 'There'll be no riding for Fran today,' he told her. 'I'll speak to her grandmother about it. You'd better take her indoors. Pat, take Mischief back to the stable.'

Pat led the pony away, while Gabriel said mockingly, 'The sultan has given his commands, and we all hasten to obey.' He swung himself easily into his saddle. 'Sorry for this storm in a teacup, Charity. See you at lunch.'

'You will kindly address this young lady as Miss Castle.' Jason's voice was like the crack of a whip.

From his saddle, Gabriel looked down insolently at his cousin.

'Do we have to be so formal?' he asked.

'Yes.' Jason was uncompromising.

Gabriel shrugged his shoulders, and glancing towards Charity, made his horse curvet and prance.

'You can stop the rodeo display,' Jason was curt. 'Miss Castle isn't watching.'

No whit discomposed, Gabriel laughed merrily. 'How you do try to deflate me, dear cousin,' he said gaily, and flourishing his crop, he trotted out of the yard, a gallant and debonair figure, for he could sit a horse as well as Jason, but Charity was, as Jason had said, not watching his performance. She was kneeling on the flagstones, wiping Frances' tears away with her handkerchief, and trying to soothe her hysterical sobbing. Gabriel had been completely indifferent to the child's terror; he had behaved like a bully. He had said he was acting upon his mother's instructions, but he had had no compunction about carrying them out. Charity could not believe that Gabriel really was a bully. He was only, as Jason had said, impatient and thoughtless. Young men could not be expected to understand the delicate handling a nervous child required. The mistake was Miranda's; she should have known better than to entrust him with her granddaughter's equestrian education. Thus Charity sought to excuse him, while she mopped up Frances' tears, and became aware that Jason was watching her with quizzical eyes. Remembering that he had told her to take Frances indoors, she got to her feet, and picking up the child, turned towards the entrance to the garden.

'Put that child down,' he said from behind her. 'Can't she walk? She's too heavy for you to carry.'

Frances, as if fearful of further ordeals, tightened her clasp of Charity's neck, and whimpered.

'Not really,' Charity gasped untruthfully, 'she's been badly scared.'

Jason overtook her and unwinding Frances' arms, carried her himself down the rough steps that led from the yard to the drive. Then he set her on her feet.

'There, little one,' he said gently, 'nobody's going to hurt you. Run along with Miss Castle and learn your

40

ABC. You'll find that a more congenial occupation.'
His hand fell on Frances' head, and he stroked her soft
hair. 'Poor mite,' he said under his breath as he turned
away.

Charity took Frances' hand and led her indoors.
Jason's last gesture had seemed to her completely uncharacteristic. So he was not altogether hard and he
had more feeling for Frances than her uncle had.

One last ordeal awaited them before they gained the
sanctuary of the schoolroom. On the stairs they met
Miranda coming down. She wore a beige woollen trouser suite, which, despite her years, she carried well, for
she had retained her slim figure.

'Why isn't Frances riding?' she demanded.

'Mr Ollenshaw said he would explain about that,'
Charity told her, unwilling to describe the past incident.

'Indeed?' Up went the arched brows above the aquiline nose. 'He's no business to interfere. I gave Gabriel
my instructions. Where is Gabriel?' She peered down
into the hall.

'Uncle Gabby's ridden off,' Frances told her, who,
with the terror of Mischief removed, was fast regaining
her normal spirits, but the tear-stains on her face betrayed her.

'I suppose you've been blubbing,' Miranda said
scornfully, noticing them, 'and got round your uncle. I
hope you won't be soft with her, Miss Castle—she
needs discipline.' After which acid pronouncement she
continued her downward progress.

Frances' lips had trembled at her grandmother's
tone. Now, as she plodded upwards, she said venom-
ously, 'I hates my gran!'

'You mustn't say that,' Charity rebuked her gently,
though all her sympathies were with the child.

Frances smiled impishly. 'But I likes you,' she announced.

Charity sighed thankfully. The morning's episode
had accomplished something since it had forged a
bond between her and her pupil.

Half an hour later, with Frances changed into trousers and jersey, Charity was dutifully introducing her to the letter A which she was enthusiastically reproducing in the squares her teacher had ruled for her, Jason came into the schoolroom. That this was an unusual occurrence was obvious from the child's expression of surprise.

'What are you doing?' he asked her kindly.

'That's A,' Frances told him proudly, displaying her handiwork.

'And quite recognisable,' he declared; he looked at Charity with almost a twinkle in his eyes. 'You won't overburden her mental powers? She's only five.'

'Not till June,' came the stern correction, 'my burfday's in June.'

'Is it then? I won't forget,' he promised her. 'Miss Castle, I've spoken to Mrs Dalrymple about Frances' riding and we've hit on a solution. Do you ride yourself?'

She explained her limited experience of the art.

'But you could soon pick it up,' he suggested. 'With your build, you should make a good horsewoman.' His eyes ran over her long-legged slimness, and she blushed uncomfortably. 'Would you like to learn?'

'Not from Mr Dalrymple,' she said hastily, and he laughed.

'I wouldn't dream of entrusting you to his tender mercies,' he told her. 'I was going to offer to teach you myself.'

She stared at him incredulously. 'Why should you take so much trouble?' she asked ingenuously.

'I don't think it'll be much trouble, I might even enjoy it.' His eyes crinkled with amusement. 'But seriously, until Frances' confidence is restored she'd better have her morning session with Dobbin in the field. You could manage that? You simply lead the pony round, but she should go further afield, and I'll see about getting her a suitable mount. Meanwhile, the idea is that you should learn yourself and then as soon as you can control a horse, you can take her hacking on the moors. I know I can trust you not to do anything rash, and Mrs Dalrymple thinks it's an excellent idea.' He looked at her questioningly.

'Well, I ...' Charity hesitated. 'Do you think I could?' she asked doubtfully.

'I'll be better able to judge when I've seen you up,' he said cautiously. 'I don't want to interfere with your other duties, so would it be asking too much of you to take your instruction before breakfast? Shall we start tomorrow morning? It gets light early now—say at a quarter to seven?'

Charity recalled how she had seen him jump the wall only that very morning. Evidently before breakfast was his time for exercise. She was aware of a little quiver of excitement at the prospect of being alone with him at that early hour.

'That would suit me very well,' she said demurely.

'Good. I expect we can rustle up some spare boots and jodhpurs. What size do you take?'

She told him with heightened colour, embarrassed by the intimacy of his regard; he was plainly assessing her measurements.

Frances, who had been taking in the conversation, now asked pertinently, 'Who's going to dress me and make me wash?'

'Can't you dress yourself?' Jason asked.

'I can put on my vest and pants,' Frances told him expansively, 'but my jersey sticks.'

'Does it?' he said indulgently. 'We'll have to ask Annie to help.'

'Mrs Dalrymple won't think I'm neglecting my work?' Charity asked anxiously.

'I told you she approved,' he reminded her, 'she also thinks it's important to offer you some inducement to stay at Carne. There are no other amusements except riding and shooting, and I don't propose to teach you to handle a gun.'

'I'm glad of that,' Charity cried. 'I'd hate to kill anything.'

'I don't shoot much myself,' he told her. 'It's Gabriel

who's our crack shot. The horses take all my time—I breed and break them. I hope you'll come to love them as we all do. It would do much to keep you from feeling bored.'

'I don't think I'll ever be that,' she said, and could not resist adding, 'You've rather changed your views from last night.' For all this consideration for her entertainment was hardly what she had been led to expect from him.

'Not with regard to my cousin,' he warned her, 'and it's only fair to offer you an alternative diversion.'

The look he gave her made her heart miss a beat, while she wondered if there was a deeper meaning behind his words. Although he had declared he was a confirmed bachelor, that did not mean he was indifferent to women, women to whom he would not think it necessary to offer marriage, but it was extremely doubtful if he regarded a nursery nurse as a woman at all.

Frances said innocently, 'Will Paula come too?'

He frowned. 'No. What has Paula got to do with it?'

'Gran says Paula likes you.'

'Little pitchers has long ears,' Jason said drily. He glanced at Charity. 'Paula Stevens was one of my pupils, but she's graduated.'

At lunch no one referred to the incident of the morning. Gabriel was lively and talkative and careful to address Charity as Miss Castle, but most of the conversation dealt with the summer shows at which Jason was exhibiting. In the matter of horseflesh, the family was in accord and all three discussed enthusiastically their chances and which animals were to be entered for what. There was only one bad moment when Mischief was mentioned and Miranda said acidly:

'I had hoped Frances would be ready to enter a children's jumping class by the end of the summer,' and Charity, who was sitting next to the child, saw her go rigid. Miranda was looking reproachfully at Jason.

'It's no good trying to force her,' he said mildly. 'You

44

must accept, my dear aunt, that to be born into this family does not automatically indicate a dedicated equestrienne.'

'She takes after her mother,' Miranda said scornfully. 'Nobody has ever succeeded in persuading Julia to get on a horse. I can't think why Martin married her.'

Gabriel laughed. 'Martin didn't care a damn whether she could ride or not, all he was after was the money.'

A pregnant pause followed this pronouncement. Miranda shot her son a warning glance, while Jason frowned and Charity looked anxiously at Frances, wondering how much she understood of the conversation.

'Julia had a lot to recommend her,' Jason said drily. 'Personally I think he made a very wise choice,' and changed the subject. So the master of Carne approved his cousin's marriage to an heiress, Charity thought a little bitterly. No doubt he hoped to find another one for Gabriel and that was why he had warned her to steer clear of him. She looked across the table and met Gabriel's quizzical glance. So now you know my cousin's plans for me, he seemed to be saying. She wondered if he were prepared to fall in with them, or whether he would insist upon choosing for himself. She thought the latter, for she did not believe he could be mercenary, but he would need to be strong-minded to oppose the overbearing master of Carne.

The afternoon walk was not very enjoyable as the day had become overcast and a chilly wind was blowing. Frances led Charity downhill towards the Clough Bottom, and eventually they came out on the road that ran along the valley floor, beside a quickly running brook. On the opposite side to Carne the ground rose steeply, bisected by straggling lines of stone walls, until it culminated in the green peak that Charity had noticed from her bedroom window, which seemed to dominate the landscape. Frances told her that it was called Shutlow, which Charity thought was an unlikely name. The child amused herself by hunting among the verges for spring blossoms, but except for a few ferns it was too early for more than a few buds. The road continued interminably, and long before they reached the end of it, Charity decided to go back. Frances presented her with a wilting bouquet, which she accepted gratefully as a token of friendship. Before they turned up to Carne, they met a horsewoman going in the opposite direction. Recognising the child, she pulled up.

'Hi, Frances, who's your friend?'

Charity looked up into a pretty face with melting brown eyes, a tip-tilted nose and a full red mouth. The girl had dark hair drawn back into a neat plait in the nape of her neck, under her hard hat. She was perfectly turned out, in an elegant hacking jacket, white breeches and shining boots, as if she had just come from the show ring. Charity glanced questioningly at Frances, but the child had become tongue-tied, and stood, thumb in mouth, staring at the rider, so that she had to introduce herself, saying:

'I'm the new nannie. Frances seems to have lost her tongue.'

The girl smiled charmingly, while her eyes ran critically over Charity's figure enveloped in a serviceable raincoat, while her hair was covered by a scarf.

'I heard one was coming,' she said pleasantly, 'and I hope you'll enjoy your stay here. At least you've got the summer before you. I'm Paula Stevens and Mr Ollenshaw's a great friend of my father's.'

So this was Jason's ex-pupil. Charity was aware of a feeling of despondency as she realised what a contrast they must make, Paula so smart and trim in her well-cut riding clothes, herself drab in her old mac. Yet why should she mind? Her world and Paula's were miles asunder.

Paula chatted on. The Stevens' place, she said, was up the road leading to Macclesfield Forest. Charity must visit them one day with Frances; they could drop in for a rest, as it was a long walk for little legs. She smiled at Frances, who removed her thumb to declare indignantly:

'My legs isn't little! Soon I'll be five and I'll be a big girl then.'

'Then you can certainly walk as far as Woodlands,' Paula told her, Woodlands being the name of her home. With a few more pleasantries, she took her leave and trotted away. Charity watched her retreating back with envious eyes, wondering if she could ever hope to attain the same easy confidence with which Paula rode her horse. When she reached her room, she found the promised riding clothes were lying on her bed, and at Frances' insistence, she put on the jodhpurs, which fitted reasonably well; so luckily did the short boots. She wondered where they had come from, and was not very pleased when Frances said they had belonged to Paula.

'She got too fat for the jods,' Frances explained, and Charity remembered that the girl upon the horse had been better endowed with feminine curves than her own boyish slenderness. She was in no position to resent wearing the obviously wealthy Paula's cast-offs, and should be grateful for the loan of them. A thought struck her. Miss Stevens had appeared to be highly eligible, and with two single men at Carne, surely she was too good a prize to be passed by?

'Does Miss Stevens—Paula—often come here?' she enquired. But Frances was vague about Paula's comings and goings and Charity was ashamed to question her further. Whatever Paula's place was in the affection of either Jason or Gabriel, it could be of no real interest to her.

After Frances was in bed, a gong summoned Charity to dinner and she descended the great staircase somewhat timidly. She had put on a thin, dark crimplene frock, which was the most suitable she had for evening wear. It had short sleeves, and as she descended the stairs she was shivering. Gabriel was waiting for her at their foot, watching her descent with a speculative look in his dark eyes.

47

'The old girl's gone in,' he said disrespectfully. 'I waited to escort you.'

'I'm sorry I'm late,' she faltered anxiously.

'You're not, but we had less far to come.' He offered her his arm and timidly she put her hand upon his velvet sleeve. 'Thank goodness the Sultan has taken himself off tonight,' he went on cheerfully, as he led her into the dining room. 'So we shan't be regaled with vinegar looks all evening.'

The dining room, which was situated in one of the bays, appeared sombrely magnificent by artificial light, which shone on the long expanse of polished table, and the black oak sideboard adorned with silver cups, but whereas at lunch time it had been tolerably warm, tonight even the roaring log fire failed to disperse the chill. Miranda, at the head of the table, looked regal in a purple velvet dress: she also wore a thick woollen stole, which Charity eyed enviously. Gabriel pulled out a chair for her on Miranda's left which had its back to the fire, and she sat down with a murmured apology, while he went to take his place on his mother's right. The fire was hot on her back but failed to warm her front. Gabriel, across half an acre of table, must have been frozen.

Dinner was more formal than lunch had been, for Annie waited upon them, serving soup, followed by chicken—a proceeding which chilled Charity even more, for she was unused to such ceremony, though Annie's performance was far from expert. Conversation was desultory, but when, after putting cheese and fruit upon the table, Annie withdrew, the atmosphere relaxed.

'I'm freezing,' Gabiel announced. 'The draught from the window behind me is glacial. Mind if I come and sit beside you, Charity?' He had dropped the 'Miss Castle' in Jason's absence.

'Please come and get warm,' she said feelingly. 'I don't see why I should monopolise the fire.'

He came to join her, bringing his plate and cutlery,

and after attending to her needs, helped himself to cheese and biscuits.

'Where did you go for your walk?' he asked.

She told him and mentioned her meeting with Paula Stevens. Miranda looked up with a sour expression. 'She'd been up here to see Jason, presumably,' she said.

Gabriel laughed, 'Don't worry, mother o' mine,' he said cheerfully, 'I don't believe he's any intentions in that direction. Paula's riding a horse of his in the next Horse of the Year Show, so naturally they have to get together.'

'I hope you're right,' Miranda sounded doubtful. 'Jason's always declared he'll never marry, but he's just about reached the age to make a fool of himself over a young girl.'

'Not Jason,' Gabriel was contemptuous. 'That man's about as emotional as a codfish and as cautious as a clam. Paula tried to get him all last season, but I think she's realised that she's wasting her time. Oh, she was keen enough, but Jason wasn't going to risk having to wed her. The ladies he inveigles into his bed don't expect matrimony.'

A remark that intrigued Charity, who had all the innocent girl's curiosity about loose women. Did the immaculate Jason keep mistresses? she wondered. He had admitted he was experienced with women.

'Gabriel,' Miranda exclaimed, 'you mustn't say such things! You'll shock Charity—her father's a clergyman.'

'Even so, I bet she knows the facts of life,' her son returned flippantly, while his audacious eyes sought to meet Charity's. '*I'm* not a fish, Charity, and I'm very apt to lose my head, to say nothing of my heart.'

Charity tried to return his gaze, but the slumbrous, sensuous look in his eyes caused her stomach to flutter, and she hastily looked down at her plate.

'Is that intended as a warning?' she asked demurely.

'Definitely. I feel myself succumbing already, but before I become hopelessly involved, tell me if there's

49

some young man in Essex whom you love and who is dying for love of you.'

Charity became aware that Miranda had paused in the process of peeling an apple and was watching her intently. She laughed a little nervously.

'Do you expect me to tell you all my secrets?' she asked provocatively.

'It would save me the trouble of having to ferret them out,' he told her, 'for I'm going to discover all there is to know about you, Charity.'

'Miss Castle said she had no boy-friends,' Miranda said coldly, 'at least so I understood.'

Charity felt Mrs Dalrymple's remark was a little un-called-for, but it reminded her that no male ever had showed much interest in her, and she announced a little dolefully, 'No one would dream of dying of love for someone as plain as I am.'

'But you have charm, Charity,' Gabriel insisted, 'an old-world charm. You look like a little Quakeress with your braided hair and your simple frock. I find your appearance very provocative. I'm longing to know what it conceals,' his voice dropped on the last phrase, and she suspected a *double entendre*, but did not know how to counter it. She was unused to bandying words with an attractive young man. Glancing up at him, she noticed how long were his eyelashes and how beautifully carved were his lips. He brought his hand-some head nearer to hers, as he murmured, 'Are you really so innocent, or is it a pose? I shall have to find out. The shrubbery behind the lawn is an ideal place for such discoveries. There's even a little summer-house.'

A ripple of excitement ran up Charity's spine and her eyes lingered upon his mouth. Gabriel would kiss expertly, of that she was sure. She imagined his lips against her own, and then, shocked at her own wanton thoughts, she turned scarlet and hastily looked away. What was he doing to her to put such ideas into her head?

'Now, I wonder what caused that blush,' he whispered, 'but perhaps I can guess?'

Charity's eyes flew to Miranda, who, at the head of the table, seemed remote from them, but Mrs Dalrymple appeared to be absorbed in quartering her apple and was paying no further heed to their conversation.

Gabriel began to lightly stroke her bare arm, and her nerves quivered at the contact. Desperately she tried to throw off the sensual spell that he was weaving around her.

'Do you always behave like this,' she asked, 'with girls you've only known for twenty-four hours?'

'No,' he replied, 'but in your case it was love at first sight.'

'And you expect me to believe that?'

'I'm going to make you believe it, and I'm having to work fast, because it isn't often that dear Jason leaves us to our own devices.'

That reminded her that she had promised the master of Carne to extend to Gabriel nothing beyond common courtesy, and she was already flirting with him. Her job depended upon her discretion, so she withdrew her arm from his caressing fingers and said frigidly:

'I think it's time I went upstairs.'

Miranda looked up. 'Won't you join us for coffee in the morning room?' she asked. 'It'll be warmer in there.'

Deciding to resist the temptation of further contact with Gabriel, Charity excused herself, saying she was tired, and suddenly she was very tired. The day with all its new impressions had been exhausting.

As Gabriel opened the door for her, he asked:

'Are you afraid of me, Charity?'

'Not in the least,' she assured him, and wondered if she spoke the truth. She was alarmed by the strange emotions he seemed able to stir in her. 'I really am tired,' she went on. 'Goodnight, Mr Dalrymple.'

'Gabriel,' he insisted, following her. He closed the dining-room door carefully behind him.

'Gabriel then, just for tonight.' For tomorrow Jason would be there.

He gave a surreptitious glance round the shadowy hall, then took her in his arms and lightly kissed her lips.

'That's in token of more to come,' he said against her ear. 'In the right place and at the proper time. Goodnight, my little nun, and dream of me.'

Charity broke from him and ran upstairs with her blood pounding in her ears in a tumult of emotion while his mocking laugh pursued her.

In the sanctuary of the schoolroom she sank down upon the hearthrug before the fire, holding out her hands to the blaze, shivering less with cold than with nervous excitement. Except for the perfunctory pecks which she sometimes received at village weddings, she had never before been kissed by a presentable young man, and kissed as if he meant it. A sensuous, rapturous tide was creeping over her and she was too young and inexperienced to recognise it as the first stirrings of sex.

But in spite of her emotional response to him, there was something about Gabriel which repelled her. His behaviour towards Frances had been unkind, and his teasing had an unpleasant hint of sadism. His approach to herself had been definitely daring and quite unexpected, which made it difficult to hold aloof from him as she had promised. She had never anticipated that she, plain insignificant Charity Castle, could attract such a gorgeous creature and be kissed by him. Her vanity was flattered if nothing else. She touched her lips almost reverently as she stared into the red coals of the dying fire, trying to reconstruct Gabriel's dark handsome face.

But it was another face which rose before her mental vision, a keen hawk's face with disconcerting steely eyes, the man whose reasons for objecting to her association with Gabriel had been made plain at lunch time. He wanted his cousin to marry money as his brother Martin had done, and he thoroughly approved of the unknown Julia, who, even though she did not care for horses, the prevailing theme at Carne, had been well endowed.

Thinking of Jason, she recognised instinctively an integrity which the younger man did not possess, though she thoroughly disapproved of his mercenary views on marriage. Gabriel had called him a cold fish, and he was too austere, too wrapped up in his family pride to have any sympathy with young love so that she and Gabriel could expect no mercy if they were foolish enough to fall in love ... love? Was she falling in love with Gabriel, was that the meaning of the physical excitement which he aroused in her? It was more like a dark spell which he was weaving around her, and surely love, real love, was much more than that.

The clock on her mantelpiece struck the hour and she realised it was getting very late. Tomorrow she had to be up early to ride with Jason. She would have to be very, very careful not to betray that Gabriel had made a pass at her, for those discerning eyes were not easily deceived.

Charity was up next morning at six o'clock and bathed and dressed herself in Paula Stevens' abandoned jodhpurs.

Frances was still sound asleep when she looked in at her before proceeding downstairs. With fast beating heart, for she did not know what to expect from her tutor, she crept timidly downstairs. There was no sound in the great, silent house and she wondered where she would find Jason and whether or not he had remembered his assignment with her.

As she reached the foot of the stairs, Mrs Appleton came out of the service door carrying a steaming cup of tea on a salver.

'T' maister's orders,' she explained at Charity's look of surprise. 'He's waiting for tha oot int' drive.'

Charity drank the hot tea gratefully while the old woman went to open the front door, whence the jingle of a bit and the sound of hooves proclaimed that Jason had arrived. Handing her empty cup to Mrs Appleton, Charity hurried out to join him.

The new risen sun was sending shafts of light through massed clouds as she ran down the steps. Jason was standing on the gravel, holding his chestnut horse and a grey mare. He looked at her critically as she came towards him, bashfully aware of her borrowed clothes.

'You should have a hat,' he greeted her.

'But I never wear one.'

'It's necessary. It protects your head if you're thrown,' he told her, a suggestion which she did not find very reassuring. 'Hold the horses, while I see what I can rustle up.'

She stepped between the two animals and somewhat gingerly placed a hand upon either bridle. The grey was placid, but the chestnut was rolling his eyes alarmingly. Jason leaped up the steps into the house and returned with a velvet hunting cap. She put it on meekly under his stern regard, feeling it did nothing to enhance her appearance. Then he turned his attention to the horses.

'You'll find Lola's very quiet,' he told her. 'She'll just follow Prince. She's an old horse without tricks.' He stroked the soft grey nose tenderly. 'Come on, let me give you a leg up.'

Charity took the reins in her left hand, placed her foot in the stirrup, and grasped the back of the saddle. He gave her a hoist, and she was mounted.

'Not quite a novice,' he remarked.

'I've never ridden a full-sized horse before.'

'You'll find it more comfortable than a pony. More to sit upon.'

He ascertained that her stirrup irons were the right length, observing her closely.

'You have a good seat,' he said approvingly. 'We'll walk up the road, and when we come to the moors you can trot.'

Lola followed Prince out on to the road. Jason took

the opposite direction to the Clough Bottom, and it wound up steeply between high stone walls, with here and there an occasional tree.

Lola walked sedately with her nose almost in Prince's tail, while Charity accustomed herself to being in the saddle. Then the walls ceased and they were crossing open moorland. Jason stopped.

'Make her come up alongside,' he commanded. 'Kick her with your heel,' as Lola halted behind Prince. This action caused the mare to make a spurt, and Charity was jolted forward. Regaining her seat, she sought to restrain the horse and finally brought her to a standstill. Jason came up beside her and she looked around. On every side were long, bare slopes of varying height, covered with a patchwork of blackish-brown ling and the bright greeny-yellow, tipped with orange, of clumps of bilberry plants. Tiny blobs of white fluff grew among them, which Jason told her were cotton grass. Across the moor the roads ran like curving ribbons. There were no buildings visible, no trees, only a few sheep browsing with their half-grown lambs beside them, and at that early hour there was no traffic; they were alone in a waste of solitude.

Over the intervening moorland, Charity saw the familiar green peak which dominated Carne, now on a level with them.

'What's that hill called?' she asked. 'Frances called it Shutlow.'

'She was nearly right, it's Shuttlings Low.' He pointed to the opposite side where a long, purple ridge stretched across the skyline. 'And that's Axe Edge. Over there, where the road divides,' he indicated with his crop, a distant junction where the ribbon of the road divided east and west, 'one way goes to Buxton, the other to the Cat and Fiddle. You can just see the inn on the top of the hill. It's the second highest pub in Britain.'

Charity looked to where a minute huddle of buildings were visible on top of a high moor. She drew a long breath; the space, the clear air was invigorating.

Jason turned in his saddle to indicate the land behind them. Here the ground fell away from the slopes of Axe Edge to a medley of hills and valleys. 'Down there is Three Shires Head,' he told her, 'where three counties meet—Staffordshire, Cheshire and Derbyshire. When you're more proficient, we'll go down to Ludchurch. It's a circle of stones by the river, and it was a meeting place of the Luddites, so called from their leader, Ned Ludd. They were the rebels against the introduction of machinery into the mills, though their riots did them little good—progress had to triumph. Ludchurch is also famous for the White Woman.'

'The White Woman? That sounds intriguing.'

'Actually she's a ship's figurehead. Someone has stuck her up on a rock in a cleft in the hillside. One walks between high cliffs, and there she is, gazing down far above one's head. She's become something of a legend.'

'I'd love to see her,' Charity said, smiling, 'and all the rest of this country.'

His keen face had lit up while he spoke of it. Plainly he loved the whole area, the place that had bred him and his forebears before him.

'You'll have to explore it all some time,' he said. 'I must see what can be done about it.'

'That's very kind of you,' she said impulsively.

His gaze came back from the distant hills and he looked at her almost with surprise. She suspected he had forgotten who she was. His enthusiasm for his surroundings had carried him away.

'I'd like you to appreciate your environment,' he told her. 'But I'm forgetting—I came out to teach you riding, not to give you a geography lesson. Now let's see you trot.'

When finally they re-entered the confines of Carne, Charity felt that she was returning from another world. Jason rode into the stable yard, and she perforce followed. Springing to the ground, he watched her dismount, a proceeding that she accomplished creditably.

'Oh,' she exclaimed involuntarily, 'I'm stiff!'

'And you'll be stiffer. Better have a hot bath when you go in, but first you must attend to your mount and learn how to handle your tack. A good horseman always cares for his beast before himself.'

So she led Lola into her box and attempted to remove bridle and saddle. The straps of the girths all but defeated her and Jason came to assist her. She was very conscious of him as he stood beside her, his fingers touching hers more than once, and instantly felt ashamed of her sensations. What was the matter with her that she was so easily affected by both Jason and his cousin? Hope was fond of talking about sex-starved spinsters, and she supposed that that was the explanation, but they each had a different appeal. Gabriel was romantically exciting, but the man beside her could be a friend.

Unfortunately he spoiled the friendly image almost as soon as she had created it, for after he had told her to go and get her bath, and she was already half out of the stable, he called her back.

'Oh, by the way, Miss Castle.'

'Yes?' He was bending over the corn bin measuring out a feed.

'I've arranged with my aunt that in future you will have your dinner upstairs,' he told her, with his eyes upon his task.

Charity was glad that he was not looking at her, for she felt her face flame. Yet how could he know about Gabriel's overtures of the previous evening? An instant's reflection showed her that he could not know, but the servants must have informed him that she had dined downstairs, and her feeling of guilt was succeeded by a wave of anger. He might condescend to give her riding lessons to suit Frances' convenience, but she must not be allowed to forget her place, and that, when Frances was not present, was in the schoolroom, nor had he made any attempt to soften his command in deference to her feelings.

'That'll suit me, Mr Ollenshaw,' she said coldly. 'I'm

only surprised ...' She broke off in confusion as he turned to look at her and she met the steely blue eyes.

'What surprises you, Miss Castle?'

'That you demean yourself to give me riding lessons. I'd much rather you didn't.'

His eyes became frosty. 'Don't be childish,' he admonished her. 'You know you enjoyed it,' (she had), 'and you're well aware of my reasons for instructing you. I shall expect you at the same time tomorrow morning, and that's an order.'

Her grey eyes sparkling, she said defiantly, 'And suppose I refuse to obey?'

He gave her his rare smile. 'You'll obey,' he said softly.

She said nothing, but her lips set mutinously.

'You wouldn't like me to have to come and fetch you,' he suggested. 'You might find that embarrassing.'

With a lively recollection of Gabriel's methods with Frances, she asked with heightened colour, 'You'd use force?'

He did not answer her directly. 'I'm boss here, and no one at Carne defies me,' he said quietly, 'either beast or man,' and he added significantly, 'with impunity.'

'But I'm a woman,' she quibbled.

'Man embraceth woman,' he said coolly, and picking up a bucket of oats, went into Prince's box.

Hateful man! Charity thought rebelliously, as she made her way indoors, and wondered if he treated Paula Stevens with the same arrogance. But Paula was not one of his dependents, and he would never banish her from his dinner table; he would consider her an ornament. With a sudden throb of anxiety, she wondered if Gabriel also thought Paula was an ornament, and as she was plainly affluent, she would be considered eligible to be mistress of Carne. Did Jason encourage her for his cousin's benefit or his own?

She gained the schoolroom without encountering anyone and found Frances half way through her breakfast, having dressed with Annie's assistance. The child was wearing her 'jods' and Charity remembered it was now one of her duties to escort her charge round the field upon Dobbin. Horses were figuring largely in her life at Carne.

CHAPTER THREE

NEXT morning Jason did not take Charity up on to the moors. Instead he gave her more intensive instruction in a field on the other side of the road surrounding a farmhouse that was part of the Carne estate. His manner was impersonal and remote, but as she jogged and bounced and strove to control Lola's inclinations, she was very much aware of the blue gaze watching her every movement with concentration.

'You must never let your mount have its own way,' he told her. 'Horses, like children, respect those who can master them.' And women too, she thought involuntarily. 'You've a good seat and light hands,' he went on. 'As soon as you can manage Lola, you can take Frances out alone.'

'I don't know if I'll ever dare,' she said doubtfully.

'Of course you will. You'll soon gain confidence.'

'You're very patient with me,' she told him gratefully. 'Why didn't you teach Frances, instead of leaving her to Mr Dalrymple? He's so impatient with her.'

Jason smiled a little grimly. 'He's her uncle,' he pointed out, 'and Mrs Dalrymple thought I'd be too soft with her, but I think we're all agreed now that it was a mistake.'

Gabriel, somewhat to her relief, made no further advances. The men were both busy preparing for the summer shows, for the family was united in its love of horses if nothing else. In this connection, Paula found it necessary to pay Carne frequent visits, and since she often stayed to lunch, Charity had ample opportunity to observe the reactions of the two men to her presence.

Her jacket discarded, Paula appeared in breeches and a tight sweater which showed off her fine figure. Animatedly she discussed brood mares, foals at foot, colts and fillies, a conversation in which Miranda was quite at home, but Charity and Frances felt excluded. Charity noticed how frequently Paula's brown eyes were fixed wistfully upon Jason and also that she paid Gabriel scant attention. It was obvious where her fancy lay, but though Jason's manner towards her was invariably kind, even paternally affectionate, he betrayed no hint of a deeper feeling, which confirmed Gabriel's suggestion that he was incapable of reciprocating Paula's love, if indeed she was in love with him. Charity felt sorry for her, though she was rather glad that it was not Gabriel whom she was trying to captivate, though he did nothing to alleviate her own loneliness. For she often was lonely, especially during the long, light evenings, when, by Jason's decree, she was banished from the dining room. Her parents' weekly letter and her own letters home were her principal diversion and by no means an exciting one.

One afternoon, when she and Frances were starting out for their walk, they paused at the gateway across the road to watch Jason training a young horse. Jumps had been erected round the field and the animal, a bright chestnut, one of Prince's sons, was being obstinate. Again and again Jason put him at the jump, and every time he refused.

'Admiring the circus?'

Charity started violently. Gabriel had come to join them and she had not heard his catlike tread. It was some time since she had spoken to him alone and his presence had its usual devastating effect upon her nerves.

'Mr Ollenshaw is marvellously patient,' she said, as the colt again swerved away from the jump.

'Too much so,' Gabriel returned. 'What that beast wants is a good clout, but you'll notice my cousin doesn't use a crop. He believes in the power of persuasion. You wouldn't catch me wasting my time in coaxing, and I bet that brute would be over that fence in a trice if I were handling him.'

'But surely Mr Ollenshaw's method is best in the

end,' she said doubtfully, for Jason's skill in gentling horses was famed throughout the county. He broke and trained many ponies for riding schools and his animals were in great demand for their reputed good temper.

Gabriel laughed derisively. 'That's a matter of opinion. My methods are more direct!' He was looking wicked and exciting, and his eyes met hers with a challenge in their dark depths as he quoted, 'A woman, a dog and a walnut tree, the more you beat 'em, the better they be.'

He faintly emphasised the word 'woman' and a little shiver, half fear, half fascination ran up Charity's spine.

'Don't tell me you advocate wife-beating,' she said, trying to speak casually. 'That's archaic.'

'But efficacious,' he suggested, with a glint of white teeth. 'A touch of the whip would soon bring those Liberation freaks to heel. Man was meant to dominate his woman. Doesn't your Bible tell you so?'

He was leaning against the wall, hands in pockets, and looking superbly handsome, his strong brown throat rising from the collar of his turtleneck sweater, his jetty hair blown by the breeze across his brow. There was a suggestion of leashed violence about his whole lithe body and though he spoke lightly, his intent gaze had the fixidity of a predatory animal watching its prey.

Under the layers of civilised restraint some primitive depth in Charity's subconsciousness stirred in response. Her breathing quickened and she could not meet his eyes, but her voice was steady, as she said flippantly:

'You're all behind the times. The caveman vogue went out with the cloche hat.'

'Don't you believe it! The one thing women can't forgive is neglect. I might beat my woman, but I wouldn't neglect her.'

'No?' She was both fascinated and repelled. She glanced round for Frances and saw the child was lean-

ing over the wall engrossed in her cousin's efforts.
'Well, that's nice to know,' she went on. 'All the same,
there's such a thing as chivalry, isn't there?'

He laughed outright.

'Chivalry in the modern rat-race? Be your age, Charity, and anyway, what girl wants chivalry? Would you
like me to put you on a pedestal and ride about with
your scarf on my helm? You'd find that deadly dull.'

She flushed, suspecting he was deliberately trying to
disturb her.

'Please leave me out of it,' she said primly.

'That's impossible, love, for you're already involved,
you know.'

She started at the endearment, then remembered
that it was used even by shopkeepers in that part of
the world and had no significance.

He moved away from the wall and came to stand
beside her, looking down at her with the sensuous look
which always stirred her. Those beautiful black eyes of
his could express unutterable things, and he was well
aware of their potency. She supposed it amused him to
try out their effect upon the new nannie, and she was
finding them devastating.

'Jason isn't always at Carne,' he said softly, 'and
when the cat's away, the mice will play—you're rather
like a mouse, a scared brown mouse, though I suspect
there are hidden fires beneath that mousey exterior.
Given the opportunity, that I mean to find out.'

Charity's heart was hammering against her side, but
she managed to retort coolly:

'I think you're forgetting your place and mine, Mr
Dalrymple, and I'm not flattered by being likened to a
mouse.'

'Mice are pretty little things,' he told her. 'Your
brown hair and bright eyes put me in mind of one.
And to talk of places sounds like a Victorian novel-
ette. We're all equal nowadays.' ('Tell that to your
cousin!' she thought wryly.) He came even nearer.

'Your place could be by my side, for I believe we
have a future together.'

'Well, I don't,' she said uneasily, wondering what he was insinuating.

'Scared?' he mocked. 'You advance and retreat, just like a mouse, and you think I'm a big black cat, don't you? But you don't really want to run away, do you?'

Guiltily aware that this was true, she was seeking for an evasive answer, when Frances gave a whoop.

'He's jumped!' she cried excitedly.

'About time too,' Gabriel commented.

They both turned to look towards the field. The colt had taken the jump and Jason was putting him at it again. As they watched, the chestnut rose gracefully and sailed over it in style.

'We'd better be getting on with our walk,' Charity said hastily to Frances, as Jason walked his mount towards them, patting the horse's neck encouragingly. She could not bear to encounter him now, feeling sure that the keen eyes would divine the inner tumult Gabriel had excited within her.

He, for his part, seemed to have lost interest in her. The dark eyes had a brooding look and his expression was withdrawn and indifferent. Evidently he was a better hand at concealing his feelings than she was.

'I think it would be advisable,' he agreed, and he sounded bored. He went to open the gate for Jason.

Charity took Frances' hand and walked hurriedly away down the hill.

'Uncle Gabby's always teasing,' that small person remarked, showing that she had not been wholly unaware of what had been going on. 'He teases me to.'

'A tiresome habit,' Charity said absently, but she did not think Gabriel had been teasing her, except for his comments upon wife-beating, and with regard to that, Jason, she thought, was much more likely to indulge in that pastime than his cousin. Jason had told her that nobody at Carne defied him with impunity, and though he might be gentle with his horses, he was far from gentle with his women, especially dependants. He had indicated that he expected to be obeyed implicitly, and she wondered uneasily how long she had

64

been talking to Gabriel and if he had noticed them, for they had been in full view from the field.

She went to her lesson next morning apprehensively, expecting censure, but Jason did not mention the incident and her carefully prepared defence was not needed. Possibly he was aware, as she had meant to tell him, that she could hardly be rude to Gabriel if he sought her out. They spent half an hour riding round the training field, and he was so sharply critical of her performance that she thought he must be out of temper with her after all.

'Take Lola back to the stables,' he finally told her curtly. 'I'm going out on to the moors.'

'She won't go without Prince.'

'Then you must make her go. Heavens above, Miss Castle, you ought to have some control over your mount by now!'

She said no more, but spent an uncomfortable five minutes waltzing round and round with Lola, while Jason clattered away up the road, but when the other horse's hoofbeats had died away, the mare became tractable, and to Charity's relief, she was able to persuade her to return to the stable yard. She dreaded to think what Jason would have said if Lola had carried her willy-nilly in his wake, and began to suspect that his command had been in the nature of a test of her horsemanship.

At lunch, Miranda announced that she required something from a shop in Buxton and suggested that Charity and Frances went in by bus to fetch it.

'You haven't seen our northern spa yet,' she pointed out. 'It'll be an outing for you both.'

'As it happens, I have to go there this afternoon on business,' Jason said unexpectedly. 'I'll take you. It's a long walk to the bus stop and they don't run very frequently.'

Charity said quickly that she did not mind the walk and she did not want to bother him.

'It'll be no bother,' he returned. 'I'm taking the car anyway and you can do your errand and have a look round while I'm busy. It'll save time and effort on your part.'

He gave her a quizzical look as if daring her to fault his arrangements, while Frances gave a sigh of relief. She had feared an expedition under his escort.

'Can we go in the gardens?' she asked eagerly. 'There's a toy railway I want to ride on ...' She looked at Charity appealingly.

'That's up to Miss Castle,' Jason told her, 'but you won't have a lot of time to spare. I don't want to be kept waiting about for you.'

'Just in and out?' Gabriel suggested. 'Not very exciting. If I'd been going I'd have shown you round properly.' His face darkened and he struck the table with his fist. 'Why the hell did I go and get my licence suspended? That pig of a magistrate was out for blood and he had it in for me—it wasn't fair.' Evidently this was an old grievance.

Jason looked at him satirically, as he said, 'If you will drive like a lunatic you must expect unpleasant consequences. Actually you got off very lightly considering all the circumstances.'

In the pause that followed this statement, Charity was aware of tension in the air. Gabriel was glowering and Miranda looked distressed, while Jason continued to sternly survey his cousin. Then Miranda said firmly:

'There's no need to bring all that up again. It's all over and done with.'

'I wasn't going to,' Jason said mildly. 'Gabriel started it.' He turned towards Charity. 'You'll have plenty of opportunities to explore the amenities of the town later on. Now, if you'll excuse me, Aunt, I've a phone call to make. Be ready in half an hour, Miss Castle.'

She nodded, and he went out while Gabriel watched his exit with smouldering eyes.

'Of course Jason never blots his copybook,' he said angrily. 'Really, I wonder if the fellow's ever been young!'

'You're no longer a boy yourself,' his mother told him with slight asperity. 'It's time you grew up. Martin's younger than you, but he behaves like a responsible being and works hard to support his wife and child.'

Gabriel grinned impishly. 'Ah, but he has the influence of a good woman to guide him,' he said mockingly, 'and he's only half an hour younger than I. Twins are supposed to have an affinity, but I've never felt one for my dear brother. It seems we were born opposites—he got all the virtues, and I had all the vices.'

'Rubbish,' Miranda exclaimed. 'Your trouble is you won't try to reform.'

'This conversation must be very edifying for Charity,' Gabriel said, and the glance he gave Miranda seemed to be trying to convey a warning. 'But don't lose heart, old girl. One of these days I'll be getting a wife and then I'll turn over a new leaf.'

'I'm sure I hope so.' As she spoke, Miranda stretched out a hand and patted his arm as if to indicate that she did not really mean her rebuke. Gabriel was the one being whom she really loved. Frances, who was eyeing her uncle curiously, demanded:

'Who's you going to marry, Uncle Gabby?'

'Ah,' Gabriel smiled knowingly, 'that's a secret.'

Deliberately he stared at Charity. She rose quickly to her feet and turned away to conceal the blush that she knew had risen to her cheeks.

'Come along, Fran,' she said, 'we'd better be getting ready.'

He sprang up to open the door for her and as she passed him, he whispered, 'Wish I was going with you, but I daren't suggest that to the Sultan.'

She made no rejoinder and he followed her into the hall to add, 'But I shan't always be immobilised, and then I'll show you a thing or two.'

'That'll be the day!' she flung back at him over her shoulder, and ran upstairs with Frances in tow. Was Gabriel seriously contemplating marriage, she wondered, and was she a possible candidate for the bride? The suggestion that he had conveyed to his mother that he regarded a wife as a pilot along the paths of virtue was a little dashing to her romantic dreams. He was more attractive when he was being rakish. But Jason would soon douse his aspirations if he came to learn of them and he had said everyone at Carne was under his jurisdiction. Charity felt rebellious. Whatever his plans were for Gabriel, he had no right to prevent the young man from choosing his own mate.

She changed out of her skirt and jumper into a neat, dark dress with white collar and cuffs, over which she wore a plain tweed coat, and decided that she looked very much the governess-cum-nannie, as she helped Frances into her midget trouser suit and matching coat.

They were ready and waiting on the doorstep when Jason brought the car round. He was wearing dark trousers and a leather car coat with a lambswood collar, for though it was May, the weather stayed cold. He looked unfamiliar out of the riding clothes he habitually wore, taller and even more remote. He opened the door to the back seat for Frances and Charity to sit behind, and they settled themselves sedately, while he slid behind the wheel and drove out of the lower gate of the drive into the Clough.

'That's not the way!' Frances exclaimed.

'We're going the longer way so your nannie can see the view from the Cat,' Jason told her. 'It's a clear day and it should be good.'

Of course, even though she was only the nannie, he could not resist showing off his beloved hills, Charity thought a little scornfully, and hills were not nearly as important as human feelings, for which he had no sympathy. He drove along the bottom of the Clough and out on to the Macclesfield road. Twisting and turning, this ascended beyond the tree line, the bare moors stretching on either side. Arrived at the inn, he stopped, parking among a number of cars assembled there whose owners had also come to admire the view and partake of refreshment.

'The holiday invasion is beginning,' he observed.

The Cat was a sturdy building, limewashed over stone with a slate roof and a solid porch, above which the cat and his fiddle were shown in relief. It was neither imposing nor beautiful.

'Tourists come up here by the coachload,' Jason told her, 'but that inn has stood there long before the motor era. It must have been a welcome sight to weary travellers toiling up either side of the pass.'

The sheep, a stupid animal, had yet enough wit to learn that parked cars meant largesse, and a woolly ewe with a half-grown lamb in tow came nosing round their vehicle.

'It's hungry,' Frances decided, 'and we've nothing to give it.'

'Okay, wait a moment, poppet.' Jason got out of the car and went across to the inn, while Frances hung out of the window, trying to reach the beast's enquiring nose. He returned in a short space of time with a couple of packets of crisps.

'Hardly its normal diet, but I expect they'll be acceptable,' he remarked, handing them to Frances, as he opened the door. 'Now don't get out of the car, and don't let them into it. Miss Castle, come and admire the view.'

His action touched Charity. How did a crusty bachelor divine the young child's passionate urge to feed every creature within reach? But he had done so and they left an ecstatic Frances doling out potato crisps to her protégées. Charity walked forward a few paces beside her guide, too conscious of him to wholly appreciate the scene before her. They seemed to be standing on top of the world. Below them a much dwarfed Shuttlings Low rose from the Clough, dividing the distance in two. On one side the uplands sank to the Cheshire plain, smoky gold, with a distant line of silver, which Jason told her was the Mersey. On the other, a jumble of hills and valleys, green changing to purple and blue stretched away to a distant misty line of summits, which he said were the Welsh mountains.

'It's only rarely that it's clear enough to see them,' he told her. 'I'm afraid it'll rain tomorrow. Now look over here.'

They turned back, walked past Frances and her eager sheep, and stopped to survey the expanses of moor that were spread wide before them, the cars speeding over the unfenced roads looking like processions of ants.

'The Goyt valley's down there,' he indicated a declivity on their left, 'and you see that blue ridge on the horizon? That's Kinder Scout, the highest point in the Peak.'

Kinder was indigo against the azure of the sky, in between them and it, cloud shadows raced over the bare expanses of moors, purple patches upon a brown and green chessboard. Only in the valleys were there any trees, even the stone walls were practically non-existent on the upper hills.

'I've walked and ridden over these hills all my life,' Jason said dreamily, more to himself than to her. 'There are still places where one can be alone with the grouse and the snipe, there are parts of Kinder which even the ramblers rarely penetrate. They were my boyhood haunts.'

A born solitary, Charity thought; no wonder he had never married.

'Did you always go alone?' she asked.

'No. I had a brother—he's dead.'

'I'm sorry,' she said inadequately.

'He was killed on a safari in Africa—one of those accidents that should never have happened. Ours was an almost entirely masculine household. I never knew my mother; she died when Matt was born. My old man never got over my brother's death. He had a coronary ... but I don't know why I'm boring you with all this ...' He seemed to recall her presence.

'You're not boring me,' she said gently; indeed she was flattered that he had so far unbent as to describe his family to her. At that moment an unexpected em-

70

pathy seemed to exist between them.

'So now I go no more a-roaming,' he said with a sad
smile, 'though perhaps Matt's spirit haunts the Peak,'
he nodded towards the distant Kinder. 'One day I'll go
to find out.'

Suddenly he caught her elbow in a firm grip which
startled her.

'Look, there's a hawk!' With his other hand he
pointed to where the bird was hovering. Charity
watched, breathlessly aware of his sinewy fingers on
her arm. 'A kestrel,' he went on, and as the bird
swooped they had a brief glimpse of chestnut feathers.
He dropped his hand, as if suddenly aware of who she
was, and said distantly, 'We must be getting on, or I'll
be late for my appointment.'

They returned to the car, whence Frances' sheep,
the crisps devoured, had basely deserted her.

'You's been a long time,' she said reproachfully.

'Ten minutes,' Jason told her, looking at his watch.
He glanced at Charity. 'Not long to introduce a new
world and visit an old one.'

They took their places and the car slid forward towards Buxton.

Buxton was known to the Romans, who called it
Aquae Arnemetiae and built roads to reach it so that
their legions could enjoy the healing waters from its
spring. That same spring, known as St Anne's Well, is
housed in the Spa Pavilion, which is also the Tourist
Office, and bottles of the famous water are sold to the
unwary at two and a half pence each. The Pavilion
faces the Crescent, the town's most distinguished feature. Built by the fifth Duke of Devonshire, its arcade
is what is depicted on most pictures of the place.

Frances enjoyed prancing along its covered pathway,
as, their errand done, they made for the Pavilion Gardens and the recreational joys they offered. Charity
was pleased to see she had become more lively and
playful than at any time since her arrival. There was a
rosy flush in her cheeks, and her blue eyes were sparkling. A small boy, about a year older, insisted upon

joining them and accompanied Frances upon the miniature railway. Charity sat on a seat, watching them and wishing that the wind was not so nippy. The Gardens were a pretty place, with undulating green slopes, and clustered trees, hanging over the waterways which were filled with ducks. She had difficulty in extricating Frances from her new-found friend when the time came to meet Jason and was consequently a little late when they reached the agreed rendezvous, and she saw guiltily that he was waiting for them, looking dour and glancing at his watch.

'I'm so sorry,' Charity gasped, for she had been running, 'it was further than I thought, and Frances was enjoying herself so much.'

'No need to rush, you're not really late,' he said with unexpected amiability. 'I was finished earlier than I expected. Would you like some tea?'

'Oh, yes, please,' she exclaimed, controlling her astonishment at this unexpected offer.

He took them into a café and ordered tea, scones and cakes. When it came, he signed to her to pour out. Frances eyed the operation solemnly.

'Just like you were my mummy and daddy,' she said happily, while she chose a bilious-looking pastry.

Charity hoped she had not blushed as Jason gave her an enigmatical look.

'No doubt I look like Daddy,' he said drily to Frances, 'but Charity looks more like your elder sister.'

At this use of her first name, Charity did blush, and exclaimed impulsively:

'But you're not that old,' and was appalled at her own presumption.

'Think not?' he asked with his charming smile, 'but I don't believe in May and October unions. If I married a young girl, in twenty years' time ...' He broke off and shrugged meaningly.

'So if you ever did marry you'd choose a middle-aged woman?' she suggested daringly.

'Naturally, if I ever married.' He took a scone. 'I'm all for a quiet life.'

So his feelings towards Paula, and herself, if he had any in that direction were entirely paternal, but she rejected the image of a father-figure. He was—what? About thirty-five? And by no means old enough to be her parent. The age complex was in his mental outlook, not his years, which he carried so lightly. But he must seem terribly young and naïve to him if he classed her with Frances. Rather to her surprise he began to question her about her home and family.

'I think you told me you have two sisters, but haven't you a brother?' And when she said she had not, he told her that she had missed a very nice relationship. The blue eyes had softened, and she guessed he was thinking of the lost Matt.

'But you've no sisters,' she said, 'so you've missed something too,' and wondered if he had. Faith and Hope had been more repressive than affectionate.

'My loss,' he agreed, and Frances, now on her third cake, announced:

'Uncle Gabby's my daddy's brother, but my daddy says he'd be no loss.'

'I'm sure your daddy didn't mean that,' Jason said repressively, though his expression suggested full agreement with Martin. Frances said nothing, but her lips drooped sulkily.

'I gather Frances' father isn't a bit like his brother,' Charity said, eager to talk about Gabriel.

'Not in the least,' Jason told her. 'You couldn't find two young men more different either in temperament or looks. Martin takes after the Ollenshaws. It's strange to find such diversity in twins, but they weren't identical. It's almost as though Gabriel were a changeling.'

'But ... but surely that couldn't happen?' she asked, remembering that Gabriel himself had said he was the dark half of Martin.

'Of course not, but ...' He broke off, looking at her thoughtfully, and she had the impression that he was about to make some revelation concerning Gabriel, but apparently he changed his mind, for all he did was

73

to ask for another cup of tea. Plainly he was antagonistic to his cousin, but that, she surmised, was due to the difference in their characters. Gabriel was so gay and irresponsible, Jason so self-contained.

When they reached the car, he asked her if she would like to sit in front. Surprised, she stammered:

'If ... if Frances doesn't mind.'

'If she does she'll have to lump it,' he returned.

'I likes to ride in front,' Frances announced.

'No, you don't, young lady, you're safer in the back,' he told her, and propelled her into the rear seat.

Definitely safer, Charity thought as she fastened her safety belt. She found the close proximity to Jason oddly agitating. He did not possess Gabriel's facile charm, but he was not without his own type of fascination. His tanned hands upon the wheel were strong and sure, he always smelt of leather and soap, the aroma of an outdoor man. There was something very reassuring about him; he would be a rock to lean on in an emergency. Though Gabriel stirred her senses, Jason was the type of man to inspire love ... Almost angrily Charity checked her thoughts. Gabriel's attentions were turning her head. It was crazy to think of the tender emotion in connection with her companion. He had probably never experienced it and never would, and certainly he would waste no romantic thoughts upon Frances' nannie, whom he had practically told was too young to be interesting. He was as inaccessible as the North Pole and about as cold. He had unbent towards her that afternoon, but it was only to compensate her for her long lonely evenings upstairs, a solitude to which he had condemned her without compunction.

Remembering that, and the reason for it, she was able to whip up sufficient resentment to counteract the softening she had felt towards him.

Jason talked impersonally about the shows he had attended and the animals he hoped would do well that summer. He would shortly be exhibiting at one in Cheshire which she would be able to attend.

'And me,' Frances piped up from the back.

'And of course you,' he returned.

He and Paula would also be performing in the Horse of the Year Show in the autumn, which she would be able to watch on television.

'That'll be delightful,' she said, trying not to sound sarcastic. The thought of watching him with Paula did not arouse any great enthusiasm.

He did not return by the Cat and Fiddle, turning off before he reached it on to the Congleton road, which was the direct route to Carne.

Mist lay over the distances now, the sinking sun filling the air with a golden glow against which the hills were dark, and faintly forbidding.

A bare, bleak country and a bleak lonely man, but both had a charm and fascination uniquely their own.

Next morning Jason did not give Charity a riding lesson, but he came into the field while she was leading a bored Frances on Dobbin, who could scarcely be persuaded to break into a trot. Not that Charity was sorry, she felt tired and unwilling to run beside her charge.

Jason was leading a pretty bay pony harnessed with a new saddle and bridle. He beckoned to them to approach him.

'Your birthday present, Fran,' he said. 'I know it's a little premature, but it's time Dobbin was retired permanently.'

Frances looked apprehensively at her new acquisition.

'I didn't want a pony,' she declared ungraciously.

'This one isn't like Mischief,' Jason pointed out. 'He's perfectly docile and he's your very own. Not many little girls have a pony like this of their own. Besides, think how nice you'll look on his back.'

Somewhat reluctantly Frances was persuaded to change her mount. The new pony ambled gently along, responding to the slightest touch on its rein. Frances, who could ride a great deal better than she pretended she could, began to perk up. The new tack pleased her if the pony did not.

'It's nice, Uncle Jas,' she conceded, for that was what she called him, though he was not her uncle.

'Good: and now Miss Castle is proficient, you'll be able to go out on the moors every morning. You must be sick of this field.'

Frances looked dubiously at Charity. 'I'd rather go with you.'

'Unfortunately I can't spare the time,' Jason told her. 'There are so many other things I have to do, but I'll come with you tomorrow. We'll all go out together and see how you and your nannie get along.'

Charity marvelled at his good nature, for it would be exceedingly tedious for him to have to keep pace with the child.

When Gabriel heard of the arrangement, as he did during lunch, he suggested joining them, but Jason vetoed that.

'You've no patience with this sort of expedition,' he said firmly. 'I don't want either of my pupils scared. Neither do I want you to go with them upon any future morning. Is that understood?'

As always when Jason asserted himself, Gabriel concurred.

'Oh, quite,' he said airily. 'I don't enjoy riding with novices. I only suggested coming along to be helpful.' He winked at Charity. 'I know when I'm *de trop*.'

'What the hell do you mean by that?' Jason rasped.

'Jason!' Miranda rebuked him.

He ignored her; his eyes were fixed balefully upon the younger man.

'Nothing at all,' Gabriel said sweetly. 'But does the cap fit?'

Jason relaxed. 'You don't know what you're saying half the time,' he complained, and changed the subject.

It was a fine bright morning when the trio clattered up the road in holiday spirits, Frances sitting her new pony bravely and Charity felt unusually confident. Out on the moors, Jason selected a smooth stretch and urged the beasts to a gentle canter, the easiest pace to sit. Frances shouted with delight and when they dropped back into a walk, Charity stared at her in amazement.

'I galloped!' the child cried excitedly. 'I galloped and I didn't tumble off!'

'Well done, little 'un,' Jason encouraged her. 'You'll have something to tell your gran when you get back.'

He looked round with a quick frown as he caught sight of two riders coming towards them at a hand gallop—Gabriel and Paula Stevens. They pulled up as they reached them, and Gabriel cried:

'Sorry to butt in on the nursery party, but Paula wanted to see you urgently, Jas, so I thought we'd better come and look for you.'

'Right, we'll come back,' Jason said, watching Frances anxiously, afraid the new pony might become excited by the cavalcade. 'You go ahead with Gabriel,' he told Paula. 'We'll follow.'

But that arrangement did not suit Miss Stevens. She had nodded amicably to Charity and Frances, but as they set off towards Carne, she reined back her spirited-looking steed to allow Jason to catch up with her. Charity and Frances were behind him and Gabriel ranged up alongside Lola. He leaned over towards Charity to say: 'This is like a funeral procession. Leave the kid to follow them and come with me.'

'I can't do that,' she replied, anxiously eyeing Gabriel's mount, which was pulling against its bit and threatened to barge into Frances' pony.

'Must you always be so conscientious?' he jibed. 'You can pretend Lola bolted and you couldn't stop her. Come on, Charity.'

'Mr Dalrymple, please do as Mr Ollenshaw said and go on ahead,' she said firmly.

As once before, she saw a devil look out of his eyes. He raised his right arm. Whether he actually struck Lola or whether something startled her, Charity was never quite certain, but she thought she heard the thud of his crop as it descended upon the mare's rump.

Unused to such treatment, the usually placid animal swerved so sharply that she was unseated, and before she could fully recover herself, Lola set off at a head-long gallop. Charity could not check her, for all her efforts were concentrated upon staying upon her back, and she shamelessly clung to the pommel of her saddle.

They were traversing a rough piece of ground strewn with stones, and Lola stumbled, coming down with a crash. Luckily for herself, Charity was flung clear of the threshing hooves, but she struck her head upon a stone and she knew no more.

Slowly consciousness returned and through the veils of mist that swirled before her eyes, she became aware that someone was holding her and touching her head with light, deft fingers to ascertain her hurt. She tried to see who it was, but her eyes would not focus and she closed them again, feeling dizzy and sick.

She leaned back thankfully against the stalwart shoulder supporting her, and felt the rough wool of a sweater against her cheek. The man shifted a little to ease her into a more comfortable position, and she felt, or thought she felt, his lips against her uninjured temple, while he murmured in a voice vibrant with anxiety:

'Charity, are you all right? Little one ...'

She smiled faintly. There was only one person whom her rescuer could be, and she was intensely moved by the tenderness in that low murmur. This was love as she had dreamed of it, kind and compassionate, not fierce and demanding. She had not dared to hope he was capable of such gentleness.

She made a slight movement to snuggle closer, while she murmured faintly:

'Gabriel ... darling ...'

The arms which held her tightened, then went slack.

'Gabriel's gone to fetch Pat and the car,' Jason told her, and his voice was hard and cold. 'They'll be here in a moment.'

Dismay and disappointment overwhelmed her. What awful *faux pas* had she committed? Her eyes flew open and in spite of the hurt of the light, she stared about her.

She saw that Lola had struggled to her feet and was sniffing at the heather, but there was no one else in sight. Jason was kneeling beside her, supporting her in his arms. It was his sweater against which her cheek was pressed, not Gabriel's, but Jason could not have spoken in that tender tone, nor would he dream of kissing her.

It must have been a crazy illusion of her numbed brain. But she had responded to her fantasy, uttering Gabriel's name, and what would he think of that? Possibly she had not spoken audibly, fervently she hoped not.

'I ... I'm all bewildered,' she said faintly, trying to excuse her lapse. 'What happened?'

'Lola fell and threw you,' he told her.

'But Frances ...' she gasped, for she could see no sign of the child.

'Paula has taken her home,' Jason said curtly. 'She's all right.'

Charity sensed that he was very angry, but that might be because she had let Lola down. If the horse had marked her knees, it meant that her value would be depreciated. But why had the usually quiet mare behaved so unpredictably? She could not remember.

'I couldn't help it,' she apologised. 'For some reason Lola bolted.'

'Don't trouble yourself about that now,' he said almost roughly. 'How's your head?'

She realised it was throbbing painfully. 'It ... hurts.'

'I'm not surprised. You've a lump coming up as big as a pigeon's egg. However, I don't think you've broken any bones, thank goodness.'

A car came bumping towards them over the uneven ground and halted beside them. Pat jumped out of the driving seat, while Paula and Gabriel emerged from the back. Gabriel's voice, light and quite unconcerned, reached her:

'We've brought the first aid kit and wood for splints.

What's the damage? Want the brandy?'

'I fancy she's only bumped her head,' Jason told him, 'but as we can't be sure, no brandy. She's conscious now and seems able to focus, though she did wander a bit.'

So he had heard her whispered words. Charity sat up abruptly, trying to disengage herself from Jason's hold.

'I'm all right,' she said. The ground seemed to come up and hit her and she collapsed again into his arms.

'You're certainly not all right,' he reproved her. 'Lie still, and don't talk.'

He proceeded to give his orders. Pat was to lead Lola home, she was lame, having strained her fetlock. He would drive the car. Paula would go in the back of it with Charity. Very carefully and gently he picked her up and carried her across to the vehicle, laying her down on the rear seat. Paula got in beside her and took Charity's head upon her knees.

'Try not to let her be jolted,' he cautioned Paula.

Something in his face nettled the other girl.

'Cheer up, Jason,' she said mockingly. 'She's not going to die.'

The two men entered the front of the car and very carefully Jason inched it back on to the road.

Remembering her charge, Charity asked again: 'Frances?'

'Oh, she's fine,' Paula said reassuringly. 'She went racing in to tell her grandmother that she'd galloped. Luckily she didn't come off like you did.'

There was a faint scorn in the fresh young voice. Charity wanted to tell her that it had not been her fault, the mare had stumbled, but the words would not come. She was obsessed by the fact that it was not Gabriel who had come to her aid. He had not been there, and he should have been there instead of leaving her to his unfeeling cousin.

When they arrived at the house, Jason insisted upon carrying Charity upstairs, and laid her upon her bed.

Gabriel remained below in the hall, laughing and joking with Paula. His indifference shattered Charity;

he did not care a damn about her predicament.

Jason took off her boots and wrapped the eiderdown round her with almost motherly care. He smoothed the heavy hair back from her face and arranged her pillows. Mrs Appleton came in carrying a cup of hot, sweet tea and he took it from her and held it to Charity's lips, raising her head with the utmost gentleness so that she could drink.

The old woman informed him that the doctor had been phoned and would be along soon.

'Good,' he said, easing Charity's head back on to the pillow. 'You'd better get her clothes off, Mrs Appleton, and put her into bed before he comes.' He looked down at Charity pityingly. 'He'll give you something to take the pain away,' he told her.

When he went out of the room, Charity felt an inexplicable sense of loss and began to cry weakly.

'There, there, lass,' Mrs Appleton said soothingly. 'Don't take on so. Many a time t' lads have been brought in off t' hunting field in a worse case than tha be. Tha's nowt to fret for.'

Nothing—except a lost illusion.

Charity woke early next morning from a deep drug-induced sleep. Her head still throbbed, but her brain was clear. Her recollections of what had happened after she had been thrown were vague. Jason had been angry, she recalled, blaming her for letting Lola down, and she hoped fervently that the horse had not been seriously damaged. But afterwards ... her brow knitted in perplexity ... he had been so kind, attending to her himself, and she remembered with wonderment how safe and secure she had felt in his arms. She experienced a little glow of pleasure as she thought of his concern, though probably he only regarded her as a child. He was always at his best with children and animals. Even his annoyance about Lola had been overcome while he ministered to her.

His conduct contrasted favourably with Gabriel's indifference, and Gabriel, she was fairly certain, had caused the accident, simply because she had thwarted him. How could she ever have imagined that he had any regard for her, or that she could reciprocate? The man was a menace.

Annie brought in breakfast on a tray, and as Charity was finishing it, surprised to discover that she was hungry, Miranda came in and expressed herself relieved to find that she was better.

'I'm afraid you aren't as expert as you thought you were,' she said a trifle acidly. 'Jason was in quite a state about you.'

Charity again felt a glow of pleasure. So the master of Carne had been genuinely concerned.

'Though of course that's understandable,' Miranda went on.

Charity stared at her blankly; she had been puzzled about Jason's motives without reaching any conclusion.

'Why?' she asked.

'You're an employee and he isn't sure a riding accident would be covered by the ordinary accident insurance. Had you been seriously injured, you might have been able to claim heavy damages. So unlike Jason not to have checked upon that point before he let you embark upon this riding frolic. He's usually very careful where his pocket is concerned.'

'I see,' Charity said tonelessly, and smiled a little wryly. She might have known there was another reason behind Jason's solicitude other than concern for a dependant. He had been activated by the fear that her injury might prove expensive. 'May I get up?' she asked.

'You must wait until the doctor has called—Jason insists.'

'Oh, does he?' Charity felt this was uncalled for. 'I feel quite all right,' she stated.

'You don't look it. He would send you back to bed again.'

Charity sighed. She did not feel equal to contending with Jason. 'Where's Frances?' she asked.

'With Annie. She slept in her room last night so you wouldn't be disturbed. She's being a thorough nuisance because she hasn't been allowed to bother you. I hope you'll soon be about again so we can have some peace.'

She went towards the door, but turned back to say:

'Gabriel sends his condolences and warm regards.'

Charity received this message in silence.

'Shall I give him your ... er ... love?' Miranda asked with a knowing look.

'Certainly not,' Charity returned. 'I've nothing to say to him.'

'That's unkind, when the poor boy has been so anxious about you,' Miranda declared. 'Gabriel's very fond of you, you know.'

She looked at Charity questioningly, but as the girl remained mute, she went out, closing the door softly behind her.

Charity put her hand to her aching head. Miranda's remarks were inconsistent with her recollections. How could Gabriel be fond of her when he had deliberately caused her accident? Again she saw in retrospect his raised arm, the riding crop descending and the wicked look in his eyes. Could her memory be at fault, for surely he would not have risked her life simply because she had refused to fall in with his wishes? But he had not attempted to follow her, he had let Jason effect her rescue and he had not been in the least disturbed by her injury. He had been flirting happily with Paula when she had been carried in. Mrs Dalrymple must have been as much deceived by his provocative words and glances as she herself had been. Gabriel cared even less about her than Jason did, for the latter had been kind, though she had been absurdly disappointed to learn what had motivated him.

She sighed and turned the uninjured side of her head to the coolness of her pillow, aware of a desperate longing for her home, away from this complicated family and the strange new emotions that had been born in her. Life at home had been placid and secure, safe in the shelter of her parents' love.

Then she remembered Frances, who also was far from her home, and through no fault of her own had been banished to a maid's room until she recovered. Frances was the reason for her presence at Carne, and the child needed her.

She would waste no more time and energy fretting over her emotional involvements, but do all she could to hasten her recovery so that she could devote herself entirely to her charge.

CHAPTER FOUR

CHARITY came down to lunch upon the following day. Her head still hurt and she had several painful bruises, but she was tired of the solitude of her bedroom and anxious to resume contact with Frances. The doctor had suggested a precautionary X-ray, which she had declared unnecessary and as he was satisfied himself that her skull had sustained no injury he did not insist.

It was a wet, gloomy day with the hills obscured by drifting grey clouds, a melancholy day that suited her mood. Gabriel no longer presented a challenge and a temptation. He had shown himself to be not only indifferent to her wellbeing, but a menace. Jason too was indifferent to her personally; his solicitude had been explained by Miranda's revelation of his concern about damages.

She took her place beside Frances, who greeted her ecstatically.

'Oh, Nannie, I's so glad you're well again! I thought you was deaded.'

'Don't be ridiculous,' her grandmother quenched her. 'I told you repeatedly that Miss Castle was in no danger and there was no need to carry on as you've been doing. Now be quiet and get on with your dinner.'

Surreptitiously, Charity pressed the child's knee sympathetically under cover of the tablecloth and Frances gave her a watery smile before addressing herself to the food upon her plate. Looking up, Charity saw Jason was watching them with a slight smile edging his lips. He asked her perfunctorily if she were sure that she felt fit to resume her duties, and she replied that she was equal to them.

'It's a pity you couldn't remount at once,' he observed. 'I'm afraid this accident may have affected your nerve.' For in equestrian lore, the rider should immediately resume his saddle after a toss to prevent such an eventuality.

'I expect I'll be all right,' she told him, though the thought of Lola aroused no great enthusiasm. It was typical of Jason to make her riding paramount, but a relief that he was not going to veto further efforts.

She was aware that Gabriel was also watching her, but she refused to meet his dark, eloquent eyes, and when he spoke to her she answered coldly. There was no excuse for his conduct upon that memorable day.

The conversation soon drifted away from her. Jason was concluding a deal with a Frenchman, a certain Monsieur Briand, who had offered a fabulous sum for one of his stallions, and he was concerned with the best way in which to deliver the animal.

'I'm sure nothing short of personally escorting the brute will satisfy you,' Gabriel suggested. 'Otherwise you'll be worrying that someone is frightening the precious cargo.'

There was a hint of sarcasm in his voice, but a gleam of triumph in his eyes. With Jason absent from Carne there would be no one to supervise his conduct.

'I'm considering going with him,' Jason returned, but gave no hint of what his decision would be.

Since it was too wet to go out, Charity retired with Frances to the schoolroom after the meal and settled her at the table with her paints. The child soon became absorbed in daubing gay colours over a large sheet of paper.

Someone tapped on the door and without waiting for an invitation walked in, and Charity saw to her astonishment that it was Gabriel. It was generally understood that the schoolroom was out of bounds for him, and she knew that the servants reported his movements to his cousin. Both of them resented this surveillance, which made Charity feel she was in purdah. It was another instance of Jason's overbearing arrogance, and she had often wondered why Gabriel submitted to his interdicts. Gabriel was by no means meek and she could only surmise that Jason's hold over him was financial.

However, this afternoon, Gabriel had decided to defy his cousin's orders. His bearing was a mixture of defiance and apology. Charity wondered if he was about to explain his behaviour during the ride and steeled herself accordingly. She did not see how he could offer any plausible excuse for it.

Frances raised a paint-smeared face to stare disapprovingly at her uncle.

'What's you come for?' she demanded.

'To see your artistic creations,' he returned lightly. 'My word, Fran, that's a remarkable effort in self-expression, but I hope it isn't a true picture of your emotional condition.'

Frances gave him a puzzled stare. 'It's finished,' she announced. 'What'll I do now?'

Gabriel put another sheet of paper in front of her. 'Paint your impressions of Carne in the rain,' he suggested.

'Can't,' said Frances, wondering what he meant.

'It's easy. Great big drops, lots of them, falling from the sky.'

Inspired by this idea, Frances proceeded to cover the sheet with large splodges, her tongue coming out to assist her busy fingers.

Gabriel crossed the room to where Charity was sitting sewing in an easy chair by the hearth, and leaned over the back of it, his face only inches from her hair. She tried to continue sewing, but as she only pricked her fingers, she let the work fall into her lap, while against her will, the excitement his proximity always aroused in her began to agitate her.

'I hope you've come to apologise,' she said severely. 'Not that I've any intention of forgiving you.'

'You'll break my heart, but what have I done?'

'Didn't you hit Lola to make her bolt?' she asked, twisting her head to look up at him, her grey eyes accusing.

'Charity! As if I'd dream of doing such a thing.'

'But I saw you raise your arm ...' she began uncertainly.

He blinked and turned away; an admission of guilt, she thought. Then he was in front of her, kneeling upon one knee, his hands seeking hers.

'Charity, you had a bump on your head. You can't remember clearly what happened. I swear I never touched Lola. A bird must have flown up and startled her. You can imagine my feelings when I saw her bolt.'

'That's what I've been trying to do.' Charity was dry. She doubted his sincerity.

Gabriel got to his feet and laughed mirthlessly.

'Nice opinion you seem to have of me,' he observed. 'But honestly, Charity, I wouldn't have caused that accident for the world, and afterwards I had no chance to help. I was ordered off to fetch Pat and the car which I may not even drive myself. Do you think I liked leaving you in Jason's arms?' A gleam of malice showed in his eyes. 'But perhaps you found his ministrations more to your taste than mine would have been?'

'I understand there was a reason for them,' Charity returned with a coolness she was far from feeling. The reminder that he had found her in Jason's arms was disconcerting. 'He was anxious about damages.'

'I suppose Ma told you that,' Gabriel said, and looked relieved. 'Rather tarnished the picture of the shining knight coming to your rescue, didn't it?'

'You do talk nonsense,' Charity told him with asperity, for he had spoken the truth. The mercenary motive had spoiled Jason's image. 'I assure you I've no romantic notions about Mr Ollenshaw.'

'So you've some sense after all,' he gibed.

Charity turned her head away, for she had been hurt by the explanation given to her for Jason's attentiveness and did not want Gabriel to suspect it.

'I wonder if you've any about me?' Gabriel asked coaxingly. His dark eyes held the sensuous, slumbrous look that always stirred her, but unwilling to capitulate to his charm, she did not answer. She picked up her sewing and bent her head over it while he watched

88

her speculatively.

'You're still annoyed with me for not dashing to your rescue, aren't you?' he went on. 'I've already explained that I had no option, besides which ...' he looked away from her and his expression became sombre, 'I don't like accidents. I was in one once when a girl was hurt ...' His voice died away.

'How dreadful!' Charity exclaimed. 'Was she a friend of yours?'

His glance returned to her and he grinned impishly.

'Only one of many, and it's a long time ago now. She was very different from you, my little nun, but then I've never met anyone like you before—you fascinate me. You're too good to be true.'

She did not like the implication that she lacked sophistication, but she was beginning to melt towards him, reacting to the attraction he always exerted over her. Noticing her softened expression, he complained:

'I haven't seen you for two days, and when we met at lunch, an iceberg had nothing on you.'

'You know I have to hide my feelings,' she excused herself. 'Mr Ollenshaw told me very definitely that he would send me away at once if he caught us ... er ... fraternising.'

'Jason's a mid-Victorian throwback,' Gabriel exclaimed impatiently, moving away from her. 'Go on with your painting,' he said sharply to Frances who had looked up apprehensively, and obediently she dropped her fair head over her splodges. 'I'm sick of this tyranny,' he muttered, thrusting his hands into his pockets, and moving back to Charity. 'Why shouldn't we be friends ...' He dropped his voice. 'Or lovers?'

A tremor ran through her at the last two words and the languishing glance that accompanied them. Fighting a losing battle against his allure, she said flatly:

'Mr Ollenshaw is my employer and I'm bound to obey his orders. Incidentally, you shouldn't be here ...'

'Oh, to hell with Jason and the whole ruddy set-up!' he cried violently.

'Hush!' Charity looked anxiously at Frances, who behind her curtain of hair was placidly painting, though a certain stillness about her attitude indicated that she was listening and had appreciated her uncle's remark. Charity went on:

'But I don't understand, Gabriel. If you dislike Carne so much why do you stay here?'

A shutter seemed to fall over his face.

'It suits me,' he growled.

'Mr Ollenshaw expects you to marry money, doesn't he?' Charity asked tentatively. 'Like your brother did?'

'Martin? Oh yes, of course. Do you think it's reprehensible to marry for money?'

'Yes,' she returned, blushing. 'Marriage should be for love.'

He laughed. 'You're a romantic little nit, Charity, but I assure you, I don't propose to marry for any woman's money.'

'Good for you,' she returned, resolutely keeping her eyes lowered, and made another attempt to sew. He put his hand over hers to still her active fingers, and said winningly:

'Don't be so virtuous, Charity, you don't know what you're missing.'

'Perhaps I'm missing what I'm better without,' she murmured.

'You don't trust me, do you?' His voice sank to a mere whisper. 'But you're wronging me. My intentions are honourable ... I think that's the right expression.'

Startled, she raised her eyes, while colour flooded her face. She met his eyes, dark and glowing, and missed the calculation in their depths.

'Charity ...' he began in a low intense voice.

'Finished!' Frances cried triumphantly. 'Uncle Gabby, come and see!'

Gabriel swore under his breath.

'You must go and admire her picture,' Charity told him. 'Since you inspired it.'

'Carne in the rain,' he said, surveying Frances' highly coloured effort. 'Very fine, Fran, it looks more like a volcanic eruption.' He turned back towards Charity. 'I'll erupt if I can't get out of this godforsaken dump.'

'What's erupt?' Frances asked, interested.

'An explosion, and your Uncle Gabby's on the verge of one,' he declared violently.

Frances slipped off her chair and came to Charity glancing nervously at her uncle, sensing an inner tumult which she could not understand.

'I think you'd better go,' Charity said gently, putting her arm round the child.

'All right.' He flung towards the door, but turned to say:

'If you continue to brush me off, Miss Castle, I won't be answerable for the consequences.'

'I was unaware that I've ever brushed you off,' she said, bewildered. 'I don't know what you want of me. We can't have an ... an affair right under Mr Ollenshaw's nose.'

'Really, Miss Castle!' He was mocking her now. 'What a suggestion—and in front of the child! I thought I'd explained that I didn't want that.' He left the door and began to pace the room. 'This continued frustration is driving me crazy—first the suspension of my licence and now you. You're my one hope of getting what I need so desperately' (an odd way of putting it, she thought) 'and now, if you're going to let me down ...'

'I wouldn't want to do that ...'

'But you're prevaricating ...'

'You haven't come up with any very concrete proposition.'

'Oh, but I will, when I'm sure of my ground.' He looked at her fixedly. 'I only hope you'll fall in with it, for if not ...' He drew his brows together ominously.

Scared by the threat in his voice, Frances threw her arms round Charity and cried:

'Go away, you nasty man, you shan't tease my nannie!'

Gabriel stared at her in surprise.

'Thanks for those few kind words, sweet niece,' he drawled. 'No doubt your nannie will endorse them.' His expression changed as he looked at Charity. 'You don't know the pressures to which I'm being subjected or you would understand. Do please forgive me for everything.'

'There's nothing to forgive,' she told him, 'and if I can, I'd be glad to help you, Gabriel.'

'Would you?' His eyes mocked her. 'I'll be taking you up on that, and maybe soon. Now I'd better take myself off before Jason comes to look for me. So I'm forgiven for all my sins of commission and omission?'

'Everything,' she declared generously, resolving to forget the Lola episode. Possibly he had told her the truth.

Having accomplished the reconciliation which he had come to perform, Gabriel sauntered away with a casual 'Be seeing you,' and Charity tried to devise some further ploys to amuse Frances, while she pondered upon Gabriel's visit.

He had implied that he wanted to marry her if and when circumstances allowed. Propinquity had brought about the situation which Faith had envisaged, but she would never marry without love, and she was not at all sure that what she felt for Gabriel was love. In his presence she became as wax in his hands, for he fascinated and disturbed her, but as soon as he left her, her doubts re-established themselves. His own feelings seemed to be confused also. Vaguely she wondered about the girl whom he had seen injured in an accident and what, if anything, she had been to him, but he had said it happened a long time ago.

Gabriel it seemed meant to circumvent the master of Carne in the matter of his marriage, and if his intentions towards herself really were serious it would give her great satisfaction to annex him in the teeth of Jason's opposition, to show the older man that though he might scorn her, his cousin did not. Her resentment against Jason was actually stronger than her feeling for Gabriel, but that was hardly a good foundation for marriage.

However, during the ensuing days Gabriel treated her with complete indifference, so it would appear that he had not really meant anything by his wild words in the schoolroom. His attitude might be assumed to deceive Jason, but it galled her pride, particularly as he seemed to be bubbling with suppressed excitement as if he were planning some reckless project which he had no intention of confiding to her.

The weather became warmer as May advanced and since Lola had recovered from her bruised fetlock, Charity was able to take Frances out every morning for a ride. Jason came with them several times to make sure that she was fully competent, but his manner towards her continued to be cold and distant. The friendliness he had shown during their expedition to Buxton was never repeated. It was almost impossible to connect this remote stranger with the man who had talked to her so intimately about his dead brother.

The Cheshire Show came as a welcome diversion in the monotony of their lives, and as promised, Charity and Frances were to be taken to see it.

Jason and Paula were both competing in the jumping events and Jason was showing a mare with foal at foot, and a couple of yearling colts. Gabriel too was to have appeared in the riding events, but at the last moment his horse went lame.

'Just my darned luck,' he grumbled, 'and there isn't another beast up to my weight. However, there'll be compensations. At least I'll be away from this dreary dump for a whole day.'

Knowing that Jason would be occupied with his horses, Charity half hoped, half feared that he meant to devote himself to her. She had never been to an agricultural show before, neither had Frances, and she expected that he would conduct them round.

It was a hot day for so early in the year. Charity wore a plain two-piece with a not too short skirt, and her head was bare. The others were all in riding kit, even Miranda, though she was not going to ride, except Frances, who had insisted upon putting on a dress, evidently fearing that she might at the last moment be inveigled on to a pony.

Jason drove them down to the Cheshire plain in the estate car, following his horseboxes—a slow progress, at which Gabriel chafed, but Jason refused to let his charges out of his sight. The distance was not great, though the hills faded to purple ridges on the horizon. They arrived early amidst a crowd of boxes and floats, delivering exhibits. There were pigs and sheep to be penned, cattle and horses to be accommodated while they awaited their turn in the ring. The tradesmen's tents and stalls were already erected and there were lines of brightly painted machinery for prospective buyers to view.

As he alighted, Gabriel glanced about him distastefully. 'Well, I'm off to the town,' he announced. 'This circus hasn't got anything for me.'

'Aren't you going to take care of Charity?' Miranda asked, looking at him anxiously. 'There's nothing to do in the town.'

'There are several pubs, aren't there?' Gabriel pointed out. 'I'm sure Charity can manage without my escort. I'm quite redundant here.'

Miranda sighed as he strode away. 'I hope he won't get into mischief,' she said. 'He's peeved about his horse. That was most unfortunate.'

Charity was disappointed by Gabriel's cavalier treatment, but Frances was obviously relieved by her uncle's disappearance.

'It'll be much nicer on our own,' she said to Charity.

Jason had left them at once to unload his animals, and Charity was a little daunted by the crowds which came flocking on to the showground. Some of them she could see were very smart people indeed. Miranda soon deserted them, being hailed by some of her County friends, and she was left with Frances to find their own way about.

They visited the dog tents, which Frances wanted to see. The sporting dogs looked resigned and melancholy, but the terriers yapped incessantly. They watched the cattle being judged in the ring, a somewhat tedious business. The animals paraded round and then stood in line for the judges' scrutiny, one class following another. Frances declared she was scared of the huge Friesian bulls, so Charity took her away to buy an ice-cream, returning in time to see Jason bring in his mare and foal, talking reassuringly to the nervous creatures. Charity thought how well he contrasted with most of the other men, who were either stout and stocky or small and lean. None of them had his springing grace and distinction.

A man next to her said:

'Ollenshaw will walk away with it. No one can breed thoroughbreds to touch his.'

She felt a glow of pride, identifying herself with the Carne horses and their owner.

The red badge which indicated the winner was pinned to the mare's headstall, and as Jason led her away, Paula Stevens in full riding regalia, boots and breeches, which were so much smarter than jodhpurs, came to congratulate him. Charity felt an absurd pang of something like jealousy, for Paula could meet Jason on his own ground, she would know exactly what points the judges would have looked for—this was their world, the kingdom of the horse in which she was only the rawest of amateurs.

Tired with so much standing, she looked about for somewhere to sit, but seats, except in the stands, appeared to be non-existent.

Frances began to become restive and as it was nearing lunch time, declared she was hungry. Charity was at a loss. Miranda had made no arrangements about this meal, but the child must have something to eat. Tentatively she approached the crowded refreshment tent, wondering if the eats were very expensive. Snacks it seemed were obtainable at a counter, but there was a long queue. The more seasoned visitors had provided themselves with picnic baskets and retired to their cars to consume their contents.

'There's Uncle Jas!' Frances exclaimed suddenly, and dived into the crowd in pursuit of the familiar spruce figure.

Charity hurried in pursuit, terrified that she would lose her among the mass of people. Jason's head was a beacon and when she arrived breathless she saw with relief that he had Frances by the hand.

'Where's Mrs Dalrymple?' he asked, frowning.

Charity explained that she had not seen her since their arrival.

'I's hungry,' Frances said plaintively.

'Then you must be fed,' Jason announced, unknitting his brows. 'I suppose your grandmother has joined Lady Allen's crowd. You'd better come along with me. You too,' he added, as Charity drew aside.

He took them not to the crowded refreshment tent but to the pavilion reserved for exhibitors and V.I.P.s. Here a proper meal was being served with all due ceremony, and Charity sat down a little shyly at the table he indicated, thankful to be able to rest her feet.

They were served with an excellent cold meal, and Frances, who had been a little silent and overawed at first, was soon chattering gaily, amusing Jason with her naïve remarks.

'And we sawed a bull,' she told him, 'as big as a bus!'

When they had reached the sweet stage and Frances was devouring yet another ice-cream, Paula came into the tent escorted by a young man in dapper riding clothes. She spotted them at once and came to their table, introducing her companion simply as James.

'I thought you'd lunch with us,' she said reproachfully to Jason.

'Sorry, I couldn't wait,' he returned. 'I'm due back in the ring at two o'clock and I found these two needing sustenance.'

Paula looked a little surprised. 'Where are the Dalrymples?' she asked meaningly.

'Gabriel's gone off in a huff and my aunt is hobnobbing with the County,' Jasper said lightly. 'So it fell to my lot to rescue the babes in the wood. You'd better get your own lunch, Paula, if you're competing this afternoon.'

A malicious gleam showed in the brown eyes at this dismissal.

'I hope James beats you in the jumping,' she said acidly.

James laughed. 'So do I, but I haven't a hope.'

Jason smiled serenely. 'Come along, Miss Castle, I'll find you a ringside seat to watch my defeat.'

Paula looked definitely taken aback by this further attention to Frances' nannie and her eyes narrowed as she watched their exit from the tent. The place had become crowded, and Jason, holding Frances with one hand, put his other one on Charity's arm to guide her out. She was almost painfully aware of the touch of his lean brown fingers and was conscious of the curious glances thrown in their direction. Practically everyone in the tent knew Ollenshaw of Carne and she surmised they were wondering who she was, but Jason seemed quite impervious to the interest that she was creating.

He obtained seats for them in the enclosure, and Charity caught a glimpse of Miranda being escorted by a horsey-looking couple, who appeared to be V.I.P.s, but she did not glance their way.

She watched the first events, eager for the moment when Jason would appear. Today he had been friendly and considerate, almost as if he wanted to make up for Gabriel's desertion—in fact, he had treated her more like a guest than a dependant, and her heart warmed towards him. In his company she felt none of the unease that she did with Gabriel, but then he made no pretence of being attracted by her.

There were several junior contests and Charity remembered Miranda's ambitions for her granddaughter. 'Wouldn't you like to be doing that?' she asked her.

'No,' Frances was very emphatic. 'I might fall off.'

One of the children did, giving point to her remark.

Paula appeared in the ladies' jumping class, but only won a second, and then at last Jason rode into the

ring on a new horse called Emperor from which he
expected great things. Charity felt a tremor of excitement, recalling the first morning when she had seen
him jumping the stone wall.

'There's Uncle Jas,' Frances remarked unnecessarily.
His was a faultless performance and he won easily.

The horsey-looking lady whom Charity had seen
with Miranda went into the ring to present the cups.
She was, it turned out, the Lady Allen whom Jason
had mentioned.

When they assembled to go home, Miranda was
loud in her reproaches.

'Lady A. expected you to join us for lunch. Where
did you get to, Jason? You never came near us.'

'You know I can't bear that woman,' he returned.
'When she gets on to the subject of bloodstock she's
positively revolting. Actually I rescued Fran and Miss
Castle, who were roaming the field like a pair of lost
lambs, since you'd made no provision for them.'

'I thought they'd get something somewhere ...' The
penny dropped. 'You mean you gave them lunch?' She
stared at him.

'Somebody had to. Where's that fool Gabriel?'

Diverted, Miranda flew to the defence of her offspring. Gabriel had been so disappointed, Jason was
too hard on him, etc., etc.

'If he doesn't show up soon he can walk home,'
Jason interrupted unfeelingly, but at that moment
Gabriel appeared looking the worse for wear and more
than a little elevated. Charity began to understand
why Jason locked up his drinks.

'Hi, folks!' His bold glance ran over Charity. 'Had
a good time? Tell me all about it.' He made for the
back seat of the car.

'Miss Castle, will you please sit in front with me,'
Jason said curtly. 'Aunt, look after your son, and take
Frances with you.'

Frances looked at him appealingly, but he disregarded her. Miranda meekly got into the back seat.
When Jason spoke in that short clipped manner, no

one disobeyed him.

Gabriel shrugged and followed his mother and the reluctant Frances, while Charity shyly took the front seat. Jason slid in beside her, but he did not speak to her throughout the journey back; he had again become a remote stranger. Miranda tried to recount to Gabriel the day's triumphs, but he was not receptive, and soon cut her short. Altogether it was an uncomfortable drive and Charity was heartily glad when it was over.

Arrived at the house, she waited only for Frances to be decanted, then with a murmur of thanks to the grim-looking Jason, hurried up to the schoolroom to put Frances to bed.

Jason resumed his old manner towards her and Gabriel continued to hold aloof. In spite of her resolution to devote herself entirely to Frances, Charity found their withdrawal dull, to say the least of it. Though Jason might unbend occasionally, she knew he only regarded her as a youthful dependant, but Gabriel had definitely aroused expectations. She could only surmise that his interest in her had faded.

As she came in one morning to change out of her riding clothes, Annie brought her a message to the effect that the master wanted to see her in the morning room at once.

As Charity hastily finished dressing, she wondered if she had done anything wrong. Her conscience was clear; Gabriel had kept his distance, nothing had gone wrong with the horses, but she felt apprehensive as she braided her hair. Noticing that she looked pale, she dabbed some colour on her lips and cheeks. Usually she did not wear make-up, considering it was not suitable to her position.

Jason greeted her courteously and asked her to sit down. She seated herself shyly, recalling their first meeting in that same room. They had not been alone in it together since that night.

'I have to be away for about a week,' he told her

without preamble. 'I've decided to take Rajah to France myself.' Rajah was the stallion which he had sold; all Prince's sons had royal names. 'Only by so doing can I be sure that he won't be frightened or injured, and Monsieur Briand has asked me to stay for a few days while he settles in.'

This news caused Charity a moment's consternation. She had begun to look upon Jason as a bulwark against Gabriel's advances if they became too ardent, but as he had withdrawn since the stormy scene in the schoolroom, and she surmised he was no longer amused by the game of pursuing the nannie, she had nothing to fear from Jason's absence. His next remark was inconsequential:

'I'm very pleased with the change in Frances. She's become a different child while you've been here. Carry on the good work, Miss Castle.'

'I'm glad I'm giving satisfaction,' Charity said primly, but even while he praised her, Jason's face remained cold and his eyes had the glint of ice. She was sure that it was not to talk about Frances that he had summoned her, and from the look of him, something unpleasant was going to emerge.

He was sitting at a small table which was strewn with the papers he had been working upon and he began to doodle with a pencil, his eyes following its movements. He was finding it difficult to put what he wanted to say into words, and Charity, resenting his unfriendly attitude, had no intention of helping him.

'I'm very reluctant to go,' he confessed. 'My absence will mean a certain amount of ... er ... relaxation in the household routine, but I hope you won't be led into taking advantage of that.'

He was referring to Gabriel, but in view of his cousin's indifference, his words seemed singularly unnecessary.

'I don't see why I should be,' she told him defensively.

'Don't you?' He glanced at her keenly, then resumed his doodling. 'Gabriel will deputise for me while I'm away, a not altogether satisfactory arrangement, but Mrs Dalrymple is insistent that I give him the chance. If he takes his responsibilities seriously, he'll be fully occupied.'

'Yes, of course,' she agreed mechanically.

Intent upon his drawing, he said absently:

'Something will have to be done about that young man. He mustn't be allowed to idle his life away at Carne.'

'Then why do you keep him here?' she asked, unable to resist such an opening.

Jason's expression suggested that she was being presumptuous, but he answered civilly:

'There are reasons why it's imperative that he should stay here for the present where I can keep an eye upon him, but I'm sorry I can't be more explicit. It wouldn't be fair to him.'

An answer which only whetted her curiosity all the more. It was on the tip of her tongue to ask if Gabriel had committed some crime, but she checked the indiscreet question. After all, it was unnecessary, Jason, she was sure, would never condone an evasion of justice.

He laid down his pencil and looked at her frostily.

'It's obvious to me that he is, or thinks he is, attracted by yourself.'

The quick colour stained her face and she looked down self-consciously at her hands clasped in her lap. Jason would have to have been blind not to notice Gabriel's sly glances and innuendoes, and he was very far from blind.

'I can't help that,' she pointed out.

'No,' he agreed. 'But perhaps I should mention that that young reprobate makes a pass at every available female who comes within his range.'

Was that true, she wondered, or was Jason trying to prejudice her against his cousin?

'Am I supposed to find that information interesting?' she asked coolly.

'It might be if the attraction is returned.' His voice was positively freezing.

'What makes you think it is?' she retorted carefully. 'Because you do, don't you?'

'When Lola threw you, you said something which indicated that you aren't indifferent.'

He had turned his head away from her and was looking out of the window. That occasion was a searing memory; it was when Gabriel's conduct had disillusioned her.

'I ... I wasn't fully conscious,' she stammered.

'No?' He sounded disbelieving.

'I can't be held responsible for what I said ... whatever it was, when I was *non compos mentis*,' she said with a flash of anger.

His eyes came back to her flushed face. 'Are you in love with him?' he asked bluntly.

A surge of indignation swept through her. How dared he sit in judgment upon her, so cold and stern, playing God in his direction of her own and his cousin's destinies?

With her eyes shining defiantly and the wild rose colour in her cheeks, she looked more than pretty as she cried recklessly:

'And supposing I am?'

He sprang up from his seat, crossed to her in one stride, and seizing her by her shoulders pulled her roughly up to face him.

'By God, woman, if you are ...' His eyes were blue flame.

She shrank from the naked emotion on his face, which she took to be icy rage. She flinched from the gripping fingers.

'No!' she cried desperately, seeing herself dismissed, Frances abandoned. 'I didn't mean I was, I only said supposing. I promised, didn't I, not to become involved? I couldn't break my word.'

'If you're lying ...' he began threateningly.

Charity forced herself to meet his eyes candidly.

'I was only kidding,' she confessed, wondering what incredible folly had driven her into making that half admission. She had wanted to needle him and she had succeeded only too well.

'Please don't send me away,' she added pleadingly.

'I don't want to,' he told her quietly. 'But you're so vulnerable. This isn't a matter for kidding, it's serious.'

'I suppose so, but Frances would be so upset if I went. I will be good.'

He smiled faintly at the childishness of her last phrase, but he continued to hold her, fixing her with a searching stare. She dropped her eyes and wriggled uncomfortably under it.

'Mr Ollenshaw, you're hurting me,' she complained.

Instantly his hands dropped to his sides and he turned away from her to resume his contemplation of the view beyond the window.

In the long tense pause that followed, she stared at the lean, well-groomed figure, the beautifully-shaped head silhouetted against the light, and noticed that his hands were clenched. How intensely he must dislike the prospect of a union between herself and Gabriel to be so shaken out of his habitual calm.

Without turning his head, he spoke in a carefully controlled voice:

'Forgive me, Miss Castle, I didn't mean to be rough, but you provoked me. You know this was the eventuality which I feared if I let you stay here. You must understand that I can't possibly countenance any ... er ... intimacy between you and Mr Dalrymple. I repeat, I've good reasons for my veto.'

She knew what they were, and again burning indignation swept through her. She was young, healthy and well brought up, so that he had no real justification for objecting to her so strongly, but she had neither wealth nor position and that made her unacceptable as a wife for either his cousin, or for that matter, himself.

Himself? Why did that possibility occur to her? If Gabriel was attainable, Jason most definitely was not. It was his utter indifference which was causing her a curious pain. If only he would be more friendly, like he had been at Buxton and the Agricultural Show, she might have confided to him her own misgivings about Gabriel, and she certainly would not have tried to provoke him. She had been motivated by a desire to show him that though he might regard her as less than a woman, his cousin did not.

'You ... you make me feel like a leper,' she burst out. 'As if contact with me was contamination!'

He turned back to her then, and she saw with surprise that he was smiling.

'Isn't that a bit strong?' he chided her gently. 'I'm sure I haven't treated you like a leper and we all like and respect you. It's only in this one matter that I'm forced to ask for your co-operation.' He looked at her questioningly, and sighed. 'I'm afraid that may be something beyond your control. You're so young, you don't realise what's involved.'

'Oh yes, I do,' she retorted, and as he raised his brows, she continued: 'I'll admit Mr Dalrymple has been ... er ... attentive. I couldn't help that, could I? I'll admit he has a certain fascination.' Jason groaned. 'You must see that yourself?' He nodded, and seemed about to speak, but she went on quickly: 'But that doesn't mean that I've got to succumb to it. In fact, I don't take him seriously.'

She looked at him anxiously, wondering if she had been foolish to confess so much, and saw that he was frowning. Her heart sank.

He hesitated, then began:

'Perhaps I should ...' but instantly he checked himself. 'No, you must take my word for it. Whatever he may say to you, he's not the right man for you.'

She wanted to say, 'You mean I'm not the right woman for him. I've no money like Julia had,' but she knew it would be unwise. She dared not antagonise him further, and she had already been far too outspoken. Instead she said quietly:

'I mean to keep our bargain, Mr Ollenshaw. As long as I'm under your roof, it's my duty to obey your wishes. I want to stay here for Frances' sake, you know that, and aren't you exaggerating? Your suppositions are founded upon something that I didn't know I said when I wasn't myself.' (May I be forgiven for that lie, she thought, but I've got to convince him for Fran's sake.) 'I suppose Mr Dalrymple was on my mind because he spoke to me just before Lola bolted.'

'I see,' he said non-committally.

She looked at him appealingly, but his face was without expression.

'Well then,' she twisted her hands together, 'I promise I'll be discreet while you're away. You ... you can trust me.'

'It seems I'll have to,' he agreed, and sighed again. 'If only you were older, less innocent, I wouldn't be so concerned about you.'

Always this harping upon her youth and inexperience, and wasn't he putting the situation the wrong way round? It was Gabriel he was concerned about, fearing he might become entangled with her.

'Do you still believe I've designs upon Mr Dalrymple?' she asked, with returning confidence, for he did not appear to be going to dismiss her.

'Good God, no, I never believed that.'

'But you thought so at our first meeting?'

'You misunderstood me,' he told her. 'I'll admit I was a little taken aback by your unconventional attire, but it was very charming,' his eyes strayed to her hair, now decorously braided. 'I suppose you considered me a tiresome old ... what's the modern expression ... square, didn't you?'

His expression was almost eager as he waited for her reply.

'I was far too scared to think anything of the sort,' she returned. He turned away abruptly, and began to pace the room, while she watched him anxiously, his brows were knitted and she had no clue to his thoughts. At length, she said timidly, 'Then I'm to stay?'

He stopped and stared at her. 'Yes, of course.'

Charity drew a long breath of relief. So the danger

had been averted for this time. She must be very, very careful how she dealt with Gabriel in future so as not to arouse further suspicions.

'After all, I am a little older than Frances,' she told him almost cheerfully, 'and I can look after myself, though you seem to doubt it.' Jason smiled quizzically at this statement, and as he did not speak she added, 'Have you forgotten Mrs Dalrymple will be here? Don't you consider that she's an adequate chaperon?' She had her own doubts about that, Miranda's attitude was still an enigma, but he must know his aunt better than she did.

'Yes, I'll speak to her, and warn her ...' He broke off at her look of consternation. Was he going to tell his aunt that he thought she was in love with her son? 'Don't worry,' he reassured her, 'I won't give anything away. She was responsible for bringing you here in the first instance, and it's her place to look after you.'

He had never forgiven Miranda for her misrepresentation, Charity thought, and wondered anew what had been Mrs Dalrymple's motive in doing so.

'After all, I shan't be gone long,' Jason went on, 'but remember, Miss Castle,' his face became stern, 'if you do get up to any mischief in my absence, home you go, Frances or no Frances—but you won't, will you?' His voice softened almost to an appeal.

'I've said I won't,' she returned stiffly.

He smiled fleetingly. 'Good. There's just one other thing. There's to be no riding while I'm away.'

'Oh, but ...' She was dismayed by this decree, she had come to look forward to her morning ride on the moors.

'That's an order,' he told her.

'Isn't it rather hard on Frances?' she asked. 'She won't get enough exercise.'

'You can both walk, can't you?' he said shortly. 'I don't want to risk any more accidents.'

'Very well, Mr Ollenshaw,' she agreed mechanically, feeling that she hated him. Proud, arrogant, unforgiving, he could not forget that she had let Lola bolt and fall. 'May I go now? Frances is waiting for me.'

Jason hesitated. 'You seem in a great hurry to be off. Won't you have a glass of wine?'

Trying to soften me, she thought, sugar after the pill.

'No, thank you,' she said politely, 'and if you've said all you wanted to say, I'll go back to the schoolroom, where I belong.' She could not resist that thrust.

He shrugged his shoulders.

'As you wish,' then he added unexpectedly, 'Won't you wish me *bon voyage*?'

'Of course,' she said, surprised by this desire for her good wishes, 'and I hope Rajah arrives without mishap.'

'He will,' he smiled confidently. 'You see, I'll be in charge of him. That's why I'm going.'

Hateful man, she thought, always so supremely sure of himself.

'Well then, goodbye.'

'*Au revoir*,' he returned. 'Be a good girl, Charity.'

She went out, closing the door softly behind her. Had he realised that he had used her first name? He had not done that since her accident, but he still considered her a child, classing her with Frances and crediting her with about as much sense. As she went upstairs she reflected that at least Gabriel regarded her as adult.

CHAPTER FIVE

Jason had left by midday, after boxing his horse—a proceeding Frances wanted to watch, for the business of coaxing a nervous animal into the motor trailer was often full of incident, but Charity forbade her. She did not want to encounter Jason again. He had wounded her with his assumption of arrogance and pride. Money and position were not everything, she thought resentfully; to be honest and virtuous in these permissive times surely counted for something, but not apparently with him.

At lunch the atmosphere was visibly relaxed. Gabriel promptly started using Charity's first name and his eyes were amorous as he pointed out that she could now dine with his mother and himself. This was balm to Charity's wounded ego, though she was suspicious of his motives. She fully intended to keep her promises to Jason, but there could be no harm in responding to his overtures if she did not go too far, and it was pleasant to be treated as an attractive girl instead of an irresponsible teenager who could not be trusted to take a horse out on her own.

She refused the invitation to dine downstairs, which Miranda indifferently endorsed, feeling that she would be safer in the schoolroom.

'Then come down afterwards and watch television,' Miranda said, and she gave a non-committal reply.

'If you don't, I'll come and fetch you,' Gabriel threatened. 'I'm not going to miss this glorious opportunity.'

'She's my nannie, not yours,' Frances objected possessively.

Gabriel laughed. 'A nannie's the last thing I want,' he said gaily. 'You haven't got exclusive rights in her, you know.' A statement which, as he had intended, completely baffled the child. 'By the way, did you know Paula Stevens is also going to France?' he added significantly.

'What for?' Miranda looked surprised.

Gabriel shrugged his shoulders.

'I wouldn't know, but I can guess. She wants to link up with Jason. Really, that girl runs so fast and far after him, she deserves to get him in the end.'

This information increased Charity's resentment against the master of Carne. She did not care if he had fifty Paulas in tow, she assured herself, but he was a bit of a hypocrite with his discourse about May and October, and while restraining his cousin, he considered he was free to follow his own fancies. If he did marry Paula Stevens, he would be in a position to produce his own heir and Gabriel would be dispossessed. For the first time she wondered what his position really was and whether he had any means of support. If he had not, it might account for his cousin's plans for him.

As if he guessed her thought, Gabriel said to Miranda:

'Cheer up, Ma, I'm not dependent upon Carne, you know.'

A revelation which answered her unspoken question, but raised another one. If Gabriel were not financially dependent upon Jason, why did he stay at Carne?

Charity availed herself of Miranda's invitation to watch television. With Frances sound asleep her rooms seemed unbearably lonely. The picture was a lush film set on the Costa del Sol.

'That's where I'm thinking of buying a villa,' Gabriel announced. 'I understand living's cheap there and the sunshine would be a treat after Carne. Have you ever been abroad, Charity?'

She had to confess that she had never travelled.

'Ah, that'll be something for you to look forward to,' he told her. 'Glorious sunshine, warm blue seas. I'd like to see you in a bikini.'

'I've never worn one,' she said, flushing under his gaze, which seemed to be stripping her. 'And I can't swim, but it doesn't matter, as I'm unlikely to go to Spain.'

'Oh, but you will, and probably quite soon, and then I shall hasten to repair the deficiencies in your education.'

His eyes were so full of meaning that Charity felt uncomfortable. She glanced anxiously at Miranda. Mrs Dalrymple, who was counting stitches in some knitting, raised her head to say:

'Jason wouldn't let you leave Carne, Gabriel. You're supposed to be learning how to manage the estate. I don't think Jason's serious about Paula, she's too young for him, so it'll be yours some day. I do wish you'd take more interest in the place.'

Gabriel again shrugged. 'Sorry, old girl, but I haven't your feeling for it. Paula can have it and welcome, along with Jason, if she can get him, and personally I think it would be an ideal match, a mating of stables so to speak, but I've got other ideas. I shan't be beholden to anyone once I'm married. Charity and I will retire to Spain and you'd better go and live with Martin.'

Charity caught her breath. Could Gabriel really be in earnest?

'You're taking a lot for granted,' she told him with heightened colour, while her heartbeats quickened.

'Isn't it a foregone conclusion?' he murmured, but he did not look at her. Instead his eyes were fixed upon his mother with an impish gleam in their dark depths.

For the first time since she had met her, Charity saw Miranda look really ruffled.

'You're being absurd, Gabriel,' she said severely. 'You know I'd hate to live with Martin, and he doesn't want me, while you know you can't do without me.'

'The hand upon the brake?' he jeered. 'But I'm not going to need a brake much longer, Mother dear. I'm going to get me a wife, which is quite a different thing.'

But Miranda's remark seemed to have quenched his

high spirits and he relapsed into brooding silence.

The film ended, and Charity said goodnight. To her surprise Gabriel made no move to accompany her; he did not even open the door for her. He muttered goodnight as perfunctorily as if he had made no daring insinuations earlier on and remained glued to his chair. She had expected that he would follow her and enlarge upon what would have seemed to be a proposal of marriage. She did not know what to make of him; he blew now hot, now cold. The picture he had drawn of them both in Spain had evoked erotic dreams, but the suggestion that he could not do without his mother was definitely dampening.

The whole conversation had been off-key, with Gabriel taking her compliance with his plans, whatever they were, for granted, and paying far more attention to his mother's response than her own.

Most of his remarks had been made with the object of teasing Miranda, and Gabriel's teasing was often malicious, but her reactions seemed to have annoyed him. As regards herself, she decided that he had only been teasing her too.

Next morning, Gabriel was missing and Miranda became definitely perturbed.

Mrs Appleton volunteered the information that he had begged a lift into Macclesfield on the plea that he had important business there, from someone in the Clough.

'Business?' Miranda exclaimed. 'But he has no business with anyone except at Carne.'

She hardly spoke throughout lunch and Charity and Frances ate theirs in uneasy silence, Frances having the sense for once not to ask where her uncle was.

Somewhat diffidently, Charity went down after dinner to join Miranda in the morning room, to find that he had still not come home and Mrs Dalrymple was obviously agitated.

'Do you think anything can have happened to him?' Charity asked anxiously.

'It's not likely, but it's so odd. He's never done this before, not since he's been here.'

Miranda could concentrate neither upon her knitting nor the television.

'If he's had an accident, we'd have been informed by now,' Charity tried to comfort her.

'Oh, I don't think he's had an accident,' Miranda declared. 'It's ...' She broke off and looked at Charity warily. 'I'm afraid he may have gone back to his old habits. It's so awkward with Jason away, and no one I can send to look for him.' She again looked at Charity. 'You see, sometimes he's rather wild.'

'Do you mean he drinks?' Charity asked bluntly, recalling how Jason kept his alcohol under lock and key. Her experiences in a country parish had included the woe caused by this vice, but surely Gabriel could not be a soak?

Miranda looked shocked. 'Most certainly not!' she exclaimed.

Charity apologised. 'But you mentioned wild habits,' she pointed out.

'Did I?' Miranda looked vague. 'I keep telling Jason the boy needs more relaxation. He was used to a gay life with lots of friends and amusements before ...' She broke off and again glanced warily at Charity.

'Before what?' Charity breathed, hoping for enlightenment.

'Well ... er ... circumstances put an end to it. He had a sort of breakdown and he was sent here for rest and quiet.'

Plainly Miranda had no intention of being more explicit about whatever mystery lay in Gabriel's past.

Annie came in to summon Miranda to the telephone. She came back after taking the call looking perplexed.

'Yes, it was from Gabriel,' she said in answer to Charity's questioning look. 'He's spending the night at the Stevens'. Why on earth should he go there?'

Her query was unanswerable.

Denied riding exercise, Charity and Frances were

playing a rather lethargic game of ball on the lawn during the following morning. It was a bright sunny day and promised to be warm later on. Tulips in red and gold phalanxes edged the closely shorn lawn, and the rhododendrons had come into bloom, red, purple and white, filling the shrubbery with massed colour. For what seemed to be the hundredth time Charity ran to save a tulip from massacre due to Frances' erratic aim, while the little girl chuckled with mischievous glee.

'Throw the ball to me,' Charity reproved her, 'not at the flowers.'

Frances' attention had been distracted. 'Look,' she pointed. 'That's Paula's car.' Turning round, Charity saw a red Mini had pulled up in front of the house—but Paula was in France. Then Gabriel emerged from it. Frances went running to meet him, but Miranda had reached him first. She had rushed out of the door, having been on the watch for him.

'My dear boy,' Charity heard her exclaim, 'where have you been, and what are you doing in a car? You know you mustn't drive.'

'That's old history,' he told her jubilantly. 'You and Jason haven't been counting the days like I have. I've got a new licence. Yippee! Now I'm mobile again.'

'But the car ...' Miranda gasped, while Charity realised that Gabriel's suppressed excitement was now explained. He had been negotiating for the renewal of his licence, knowing, though the rest of the family had forgotten, that he was due to be reinstated.

'Oh, it's Paula's,' he said airily. 'She said she'd lend it to me while she's away. I spent the night at Woodlands and collected it. Very hospitable people, the Stevens,' he grinned. 'I think they imagine I also am one of Paula's boy-friends.'

Miranda had raised her eyebrows. 'Paula must be crazy to lend you her car!'

'Not at all, she's a very long-sighted young lady,' Gabriel told her cryptically, throwing an oblique glance at Charity, who had joined Frances. 'I swore her to secrecy. I didn't want old Sourpuss to know I was in circulation again before he must. But don't let's waste this glorious day. I'm going to take you all out. Where shall we go?'

Charity's heart leaped at the prospect of a drive, for it was indeed a glorious day, one of those May days that hold all the promise of summer, but Mrs Dalrymple was looking dubious.

'You will be careful, Gabby?' she asked.

'Don't you fret,' he returned. 'Too much depends upon my discretion to run any risks. Go and get ready, I'm not going to wait all day for you.' He turned to Charity. 'You too, buzz off and get on your glad rags.'

Charity ran after Frances, who was rushing indoors to prepare for the expedition. This entailed a wash and comb under protest, and a change into a frock and cardigan. Charity put on the crimplene dress she had worn when she had come down to dinner, its severity relieved by a short white jacket that could be discarded if the day fulfilled its promise of warmth.

When she and her charge came down again, they found that Miranda had remembered that it was Ascension Day, the date upon which Tissington held its well-dressing ceremony, and Gabriel had agreed to take them to see it. Mrs Appleton had hastily packed a picnic lunch which was stowed in the boot, and they set off in holiday spirits. Miranda, as became her position, sat in the front with her son, while Frances and Charity sat behind. As they went along, Mrs Dalrymple explained to Charity the custom of well-dressing, which was peculiar to Derbyshire. There was no doubt that it had had its origin in a dim, pagan past, developing from the age-old fear and worship of water gods and spirits, whose cult demanded gifts and offerings.

'Yes,' Gabriel interpolated, 'people of all countries used to make sacrifices as thank-offerings for the gift of water, preferably virgins and children whom they threw into the rivers and springs. So now you know, Fran, why we're taking you and Charity along with us.'

'Is you kidding, Uncle Gabby?' Frances asked doubtfully.

'Of course he is,' Charity said quickly, disliking Gabriel's proneness for this form of teasing. 'Anyway, it's never done now we're Christians.'

'Exactly,' Miranda went on. 'In Christian times, thankfulness for water is expressed by holding services by wells and springs, and decorating them with flowers, but just how this picture flowering developed is not known.' She described how the old custom which had lapsed in so many villages had been revived extensively during the past sixty years, and particularly during the last two decades.

'Since it's been found to be a tourist attraction,' Gabriel said flippantly, 'villages that had forgotten all about it are digging it up again.'

'The tourists are spoiling it,' Miranda told them sadly, and went on to explain that the Derbyshire offerings were in the form of pictures made out of flower petals on wooden boards. The boards were covered with soft clay and the petals inserted one by one, overlapping like slates on a roof. Thousands of petals of different colours were used. The subjects were usually Biblical. The work was intricate and demanded great patience, but the result was often strikingly beautiful, the petals having a sheen and lustre superior to any paint. The screens thus formed were erected by the well or wells and a well-blessing ceremony was held. The village they were about to visit possessed five wells, and it was at Tissington that the custom was said to have originated, because it was the only village that did not pay its toll to the Black Death which had ravaged so many others, its immunity being ascribed to the purity of its well water.

It was a long journey and they arrived too late for the service of the Blessing of the Wells, which had taken place in the middle of the morning, but Miranda's comment on tourists was only too apt. Motor coaches and cars were cutting up the grass of the roadside and strewing the pretty village with their usual debris. They were able to glimpse the screens, some of them being in exquisite surroundings, one being set up behind a pavement in which was set a coffin-shaped well, beside the gnarled trunk of an old tree, which made a canopy of young green above it. The picture represented the Finding of Moses, and was surrounded by an intricate border, culminating in a semi-circular arch, crowned with a star within a small circle. It was almost unbelievable that the clear outlines could have been made out of flower petals. The other four wells had equally beautiful pictures, pictures which like the mayfly would only live for a day; on the morrow they would begin to wilt. The pushing crowds were oppressive and Charity was glad when Miranda suggested leaving.

'We'll go on to Haddon,' Gabriel said. 'There's a good parking field there where we can picnic, and I'd like Charity to see the Hall.'

'Is it something special?' she asked.

'For you and me it has a message,' he told her, but refused to be more explicit, while Miranda pointed out it would be a long drive, and they had already travelled far.

'What of it?' he returned. 'We've got a lot of the day left, and it stays light late now.'

The road led over high uplands, and Charity was fast becoming familiar with the character of the country, grey stone walls and buildings, green fields, brown and green moors, that would later on turn purple when the ling bloomed, the outcrops of whitish rock, and here and there deep valleys amidst the hills, with rivers along their bottoms, and sheer cliffs of white rock; the dales. Green and grey were the predominant colours and all too often the sky matched the land it overhung, but not upon that morning, for the sun shone out of a cloudless pall of blue.

They ate their lunch rather late, not in the parking field, but in one beyond it that rose up to a low hill top. Mrs Appleton had been given no time to cut sandwiches, so she had packed a whole loaf, a packet of

116

butter, a cooked chicken, lettuce and tomatoes upon which they fed hungrily. There was also apple turnovers, oranges, apples, bananas and cheese.

The meal concluded, they repacked the baskets and walked down across the road to the entrance to the hall.

Haddon Hall was already old when Dorothy Vernon, wife of John Manners, inherited it from her father in 1567. It stands on a slight eminence above the River Wye, a mediaeval building with towers and crenellated walls. One-time seat of the Dukes of Rutland, it is no longer inhabited.

The entrance led into an ancient courtyard from which they duly inspected the kitchens and the chapel and then ascended the stone steps to the main building. Here was the Banqueting Hall, stone-floored with massive beams and a minstrels' gallery; a less austere dining room, panelled in wood, and upstairs, the Earl's bedroom and other apartments, hung with occasional tapestries, containing a few odd tables and chairs. The lack of furniture puzzled Frances, who could see no point in visiting empty rooms. Finally they reached the Long Gallery. This was a splendid, light and airy apartment, with immense latticed windows upon three sides, the walls being panelled in silvery grey wood covered with the patina of age. Gabriel stood beside Charity in one of the window alcoves, overlooking the terraced gardens below, and surveyed the one hundred and ten feet of shining wooden floor.

'According to the guide book it was from here that during a ball held in honour of her sister's wedding Dorothy Vernon fled to join her lover,' Gabriel told her. 'John Manners was waiting for her down by the packhorse bridge. It must have been a pretty sight with all those people in their Elizabethan costume dancing ... what did they dance in those days?'

'I think a pavane was one of them,' she suggested, 'but they were all very stately and solemn.'

'They could hardly have performed our modern antics in those costumes,' Miranda remarked drily.

Charity tried to envisage the empty, silent room thronged with dancers in the silks and velvets of long ago, and among them the young girl who would be wondering if she were going to succeed in making her escape from the tyranny of her parent and guardian. She became aware of Gabriel's eyes fixed upon her quizzically, and it occurred to her that there were points of resemblance between her own situation and the romantic Dorothy's. Was that why he had brought her here? But she had no intention of running away with him or anybody else.

Since it was early in the season and a weekday there were few visitors, and they had the place almost to themselves. Frances was improvising some dance steps of her own, tempted by the long expanse of shining floor. Miranda crossed to the fireplace to examine more closely the painting of the Hall that was inset over the mantelpiece. Still standing beside her in the alcove, Gabriel went on:

'The story of Dorothy's elopement is what most people remember about Haddon. Why her father objected to John Manners, I wouldn't know, he seems to have been a propertied gentleman, but perhaps Sir George Vernon had other plans, and like someone else we know was determined to get his own way. Recalcitrant females, especially daughters, could expect no mercy in those days. It was imprisonment on bread and water and the whip until they gave in. It was definitely a man's world.' He was looking at her out of the corners of his eyes, and she remembered the anti-feminist views he had expressed upon a former occasion, and again a little shiver ran up her spine.

'It was a barbarous way to treat one's children,' she said emphatically. 'Fancy being bullied into marrying someone you didn't like.'

'Or not allowed to marry someone you did,' he said meaningly. 'But inclinations were not allowed to stand in the way of political unions, and it was a harsh age.' He moved away impatiently. 'Let's go and look at the gardens.'

He seemed restless and on edge, but Charity was becoming accustomed to his strange moods, and attached no importance to them.

The gardens at Haddon are remarkable for their roses, but these were only just beginning to come into bloom. They were laid out in terraces, descending the hillside on the south of the house. Upon the largest of these, Miranda parked herself upon a seat, declaring that she could walk no further. In the middle of the square lawn was an artificial pool, from which a fountain rose, which Frances rushed to investigate. Gabriel took Charity's elbow in a firm grip.

'Come with me,' he commanded imperiously.

She hung back apprehensively. 'I can't leave Frances,' she excused herself, for there seemed every probability that the child would fall into the water.

'Rubbish. Ma'll keep an eye on her and that pool's not deep.'

He propelled her towards the broad flight of steps leading to the Upper Terrace and she went, half reluctantly, half eagerly, impelled by an urgency that she could not resist.

The Upper Terrace had once been the bowling alley and overlooked the rest of the grounds. Far below could be seen the narrow thread of the packhorse bridge across which Dorothy Vernon had made her escape. Gabriel led Charity towards the house and when they reached it, they were confronted by a narrow stair between stone balustrades leading down from a forbidding-looking door in the wall. Charity looked at him in surprise; they seemed to have come to a dead end, but the spot was completely secluded.

'Why have you brought me here?' she asked.

Removing his hand from her elbow, he indicated the steps.

'It was out of that door that the fair Dorothy—if she was fair, the picture of her in the dining room looks rather grim—escaped from the ball to join her lover. She ran through the gardens down to the river ...' He was leaning against the balustrade, regarding her lazily. 'It seems to me she had the right idea. When there's obstruction at home—elope. What do you say to eloping?'

'You're joking, of course,' she said uncertainly.

'Oh no, I'm not. Marriage is far too serious a matter to joke about. At least it is for me. Surely you realise that I'm ...' he paused as if seeking for the right word, 'interested in you? I want to marry you, Charity.'

He spoke without emotion, and when he had finished, he turned away from her and absently began to stroke the round stone ball that surmounted the post at the end of the balustrade.

Charity stared at his averted face in perplexity. She had half expected some sort of declaration which the preamble about the long-dead Dorothy had been leading up to, but the denouement was flat. Surely Gabriel of all people should have been capable of a more passionate proposal?

Equally unemotionally, she asked:

'Why do you want to marry me, Gabriel?'

'Because ... Oh, for the usual reasons why a man wants a woman.' Now he spoke more animatedly and he turned to look at her. 'You don't want always to be a nannie, do you?'

'No, but I'm not going to marry just for a meal ticket,' she said firmly, and he laughed.

'You want the trimmings?' he suggested. 'And I'm not acting up to my usual form. Fact is, Charity, I haven't had any practice in proposing legal unions, the solemnity of the occasion cramps my style.'

'It shouldn't,' she whispered. 'If ... if your heart's in it.' And she looked at him expectantly, for he had said nothing about love.

He met her candid grey eyes and a look almost of shame crossed his face.

'You're too good for me, Charity,' he told her gruffly. 'I warn you I'll make a rotten husband. You ought not to marry me.'

For once he spoke with absolute sincerity, and Charity was more moved by this uncharacteristic humility than any extravagant declaration.

'Isn't that for me to judge?' she asked demurely.

'Judge? What do you know about men, you poor little innocent?' he asked contemptuously. 'To take you is like picking a lily and throwing it down into the mud.'

This exaggeration amused her. 'You do talk nonsense, don't you?' she returned, for she felt she was mistress of the situation. 'I'm no lily, I'm an ordinary girl with normal feelings.'

'Are you, love?' He grinned impishly, and looked hastily around to make sure there was no one in sight. 'We'll put that to the test. This is much more satisfactory than talking.'

He swept her into his arms, and as she yielded to his embrace, passion leaped in him and he kissed her hard upon throat, cheeks and eyes, and finally her mouth. Charity's young blood responded, but as his ardour increased, a vague alarm awoke in her and she struggled to free herself. But Gabriel would not let her go, her resistance was exciting him, and his hold tightened as his kisses became more insistent.

When he finally released her, she had to cling to the balustrade for support. She was shaken and bewildered by the chaotic emotions seething within her. Not the least of them was a surge of triumph. The possibility that Faith had prophesied had occurred. Gabriel had proposed to the nondescript little nobody and in the teeth of his cousin's opposition. She could now flout Jason's interdict with impunity if she so desired, repay him with interest for the humiliations to which he had subjected her—the enforced seclusion, the emphasis upon her unsuitability to become a member of his family, his complete indifference to her femininity. Another man had found her desirable enough to wish to marry her.

It did not strike her as significant that her mind was more occupied with Jason's reactions than Gabriel's.

He brought her back to awareness of him with a jerk, by saying:

'Your co-operation up to a point was fine, but, like the mouse I once called you, you always panic when I warm up.'

She flushed uncomfortably.

'I ... I'm a little scared ... you see, I've never been in love before.'

'And you're in love with me?'

'Why else should I want to marry you?' she asked, surprised, but even as she spoke, doubt struck her. Did she love him, and did she really want to marry him? He drew her with a strong sexual appeal. In his arms she surrendered to the exciting sensations he aroused, but young as she was, she knew that was not enough, and there were times when his callousness repelled her. She began to feel that she was enmeshed in a web of dark enchantment and to rebel against her captivity.

She looked at him. He was so very handsome, any girl's dream of Prince Charming, and yet ... Another face rose before her mental vision, not nearly so good-looking, with piercing blue eyes that could also look so kind. She had never seen Gabriel look kind.

'So now you won't object to coming away with me,' he said confidently.

A cold finger seemed to touch her heart and she stared at him in startled dismay. 'What do you mean?'

'That the Sultan's absence is our opportunity. We'll do a bunk for Spain. Ma'll supply the funds and I expect we can make arrangements to get married out there before Jason can find us.'

This wild and impracticable programme appalled her. She had never contemplated anything so precipitous.

'No!' she cried vehemently. 'I couldn't do that. If you really love me,' she forgot he had not mentioned that, 'and if we decide to marry, the right thing to do is to go to Mr Ollenshaw and tell him so. We're both of age, he can't stop us. To run away would be cowardly and quite unnecessary.'

This unexpected opposition caused Gabriel to look exasperated, but he made an obvious effort to speak patiently.

'The other way is so much more romantic and will save so much bother. Don't you want to go to Spain, Charity? Think of the sunshine, the glamour and being alone with me.'

'You might change your mind about marrying me when we got there,' she said drily.

'Darling, haven't I explained that marriage is the primary object and that I want to marry you? Don't you trust me?'

She looked away over the shimmering gardens. The truth was that she did not, and love without trust was an unhappy thing—but did she love him, and the thought of being alone with him made her suddenly afraid.

'I'm not going to be rushed into a crazy elopement,' she said firmly. 'Nor even into a rash engagement. Marriage is important, it's for always.'

'Not nowadays,' he returned flippantly. 'Nobody believes in the till death do us part stuff any longer.'

A singularly unfortunate observation from a prospective husband, Charity thought.

'But I want ours to last,' she asserted.

'Why shouldn't it, but who can foretell the future?' Gabriel pointed out. Conquering his rising irritation, he spoke coaxingly: 'Do stop being a prim little Quakeress and give yourself up to enjoying life with me.' He slipped a cajoling arm around her. 'Believe me, I need you desperately—as my wife.'

Charity quivered, but she resolutely withdrew from his hold.

'I can't leave Frances in the lurch,' she declared.

'That kid!' he exclaimed contemptuously. 'What does it matter about her?' His face darkened ominously. 'You're stalling; you're not by any chance hankering after Jason? Did his attentions when you bumped your head raise expectations? I thought you knew what prompted those.'

'Don't be absurd,' she said quickly, but a warm tide of colour stained her face and he noticed it.

'If you are, you're wasting your time,' he said savagely. 'If Jason succumbs to anything female it'll be Paula. As for you, he doesn't see you as a woman at all.'

'I know that,' she said quietly, but now she had gone very pale, while the fantastic thought occurred to her that if it had been Jason who was pleading with her, she could not have denied him, which was of course ridiculous; as well expect the man in the moon to ask her to go away with him.

'Actually I dislike him,' she added, and tried to make herself believe that she spoke the truth. 'But I need time to think, Gabriel. My ... our ... whole future is in question. Surely there's no desperate hurry? We're both living in the same house and we can plan something more sensible, can't we?' She looked at him appealingly.

'I hate waiting,' he said petulantly. 'I hoped to settle this matter here and now.' A wicked glint came into his eyes. 'If you keep me dangling, you may lose me. There are other girls who wouldn't be so fussy.'

Stung, she cried fiercely: 'Then go and find one!'

Realising that he had blundered, Gabriel said hastily:

'Of course I didn't mean that, but you provoked me.' He looked at her curiously. 'You wouldn't really want me to do that?'

'No, of course not. Oh, Gabriel, do try to understand. This has all happened so quickly. I don't feel sure ...'

She wanted reassurance, tenderness, understanding of her perplexities, consideration for her hesitation, but she was not going to get any of these from Gabriel.

His brows drew together threateningly and his lips curved sulkily.

'Shilly-shallying,' he muttered. 'I thought it was all plain sailing. You love me ...'

She interrupted him. 'I'm not even sure about that.'

'You mean you've been playing with me?'

'No, but please ...'

'Hell!' he exclaimed, flinging away from her. 'Don't you women ever know your own minds?'

He strode away from her along the terrace and down the long flight of steps to where Miranda was sitting on the lawn. Charity followed meekly in his wake, her mind chaotic. One thought was predominant and that under the circumstances was an odd one. She was wishing that Jason was home again. He would be a defence and a support against Gabriel and her own wayward feelings. Against Gabriel, whom she had imagined that she loved? That almost amounted to disloyalty, but there was no doubt that life at the Hall was much less complicated under his calm supervision.

Miranda watched their approach with arched brows, noting Gabriel's thunderous expression; her cold glance went from his face to Charity's anxious one with reproach in her eyes.

'Didn't you manage to settle it all?' she asked doubtfully.

'Unfortunately, no,' Gabriel told her curtly. 'Charity is burdened with a Puritan conscience and refuses to take the easy way out.'

So Miranda was in his confidence and approved of his precipitancy. Uneasily Charity wondered if something unexplained lay behind this proposed marriage.

'Don't play with your happiness,' Mrs Dalrymple urged her. 'It can so easily slip through your fingers. Take what you want while you can.'

But did Gabriel represent her happiness? About that she was becoming less and less sure.

Frances came running up declaring excitedly that she had seen a fish, and Charity was saved the necessity of making any rejoinder to this uncharacteristic remark.

They went back out of the old-world garden with its romantic associations which had failed to influence Charity to make the decision which Gabriel wanted, to find their car. As they reached the bottom of the gardens, Charity glanced back at the narrow stone bridge where another girl had fled to happiness and gave an involuntary sigh. Had she been over-cautious, over-dutiful not to snatch what had been offered to her? Dorothy Vernon could have had no qualms when she embarked upon her flight, but in her own case she was full of misgivings.

On the long drive home, Gabriel talked animatedly to his mother, ignoring Charity's presence in the back seat, while Frances fell asleep with her head in her lap.

Charity sat alone in the schoolroom watching the day-light fade. Her dinner had been sent up to her as usual, though at a later hour owing to their late return, and she had not gone downstairs to watch television for she wanted to be alone.

Gabriel was angry with her as he always was with anyone who opposed him, and had made no attempt to persuade her to join him. She was dazzled by his charm, thrilled by his embraces, flattered by his wish to marry her, but for all that, some deep underlying instinct was warning her that she was mistaking desire for love, and she could never be happy with him.

Moreover, she did not like deceit and could see no reason for it, unless Gabriel was hiding some secret from her which he feared his cousin might disclose. That possibility had occurred to her more than once to account for the hold Jason appeared to have over Gabriel. The master of Carne was not an ogre, merely a proud, arrogant man who liked to have his own way: old-fashioned too, for nobody cared about mesalliances nowadays, but Jason made a fetish of his family.

The honest course was for Gabriel to declare his intentions openly, and Charity was humiliated and puzzled by his refusal to do so. Jason would immediately dismiss her, but that need not part them, and her courtship could proceed along normal lines. Gabriel could presumably visit her at home, though the thought of him at Maytree was oddly incongruous. He would be a bird of paradise among sparrows, but he had chosen a sparrow to be his mate.

The sparrow, however, though fully alive to the honour being done to her, was having difficulty in sorting out her feelings in connection with him. She was doubtful if she could ever do so as long as she was in daily contact with him. It might be a wise move to return home on her own initiative without waiting to be evicted.

Away from Carne and its conflicting influences, she would be more able to come to a decision, and if it were unfavourable to Gabriel's suit, it would be easier to inform him through the post than have to face his stormy rage, the very thought of which terrified her.

CHAPTER SIX

NEXT morning after breakfast, Miranda came to see if Charity wanted anything from Macclesfield as she was going shopping with her son. She made no reference to the events of the previous day and was her usual aloof self.

After they had gone, Charity took Frances downstairs to play in the garden, and as they reached the foot of the stairs, the telephone rang.

Charity hesitated: it was not her place to take messages, but she knew that Mrs Appleton hated answering the phone, regarding it as an invention of the devil. The bell rang again stridently, and sure enough, when Mrs Appleton appeared, she asked her to see who it was.

'My hearing not being what it was.'

Charity lifted off the receiver, and hearing Jason's voice, she nearly dropped it. She told him both the Dalrymples had gone out in the car.

'Car? What car?' he demanded.

'Mr Dalrymple's borrowed one.'

'Borrowed? Oh, good lord, what a forgetful idiot I've been!' He had recollected that Gabriel was due for reinstatement. 'It's certainly time I came back. This is to advise you that I'll be home the day after tomorrow. Being a good girl?'

Somehow she forced out an affirmation; this was not the time for revelations.

'Fine! Goodbye, Charity, be seeing you.'

He seemed in good spirits, and had addressed her informally. She cradled the receiver with trembling fingers, feeling overwhelmed by guilt. His voice, quick and clipped, had brought him forcibly before her, the lean strength of him and the keen look in his eyes. It would be very hard to tell him that she was leaving him.

As they went out into the sunshine, Frances asked eagerly:

'Was that Uncle Jas? Is he coming home?'

'The day after tomorrow.'

'Oh, goody!' Frances skipped. 'Then we can go riding again.'

Charity realised that she also was glad Jason was returning. She had missed the riding, but she had also missed the presence of the master of Carne. She wondered if she dared tell him that Gabriel had been importuning her, and ask for his protection. But she was certain that Gabriel would retaliate by declaring that she had encouraged him, and up to a point she had. If she did not want to find herself in an embarrassing situation, she had no option but to leave, much though she disliked deserting Frances.

If Charity was secretly pleased by the news of Jason's advent, the Dalrymples were filled with consternation.

'I thought he'd stay on a bit longer, especially as Paula is with him,' Gabriel said glumly, and Charity experienced a little stab; she had forgotten Paula was sharing Jason's visit to France.

'There's still one day of grace,' he went on, looking significantly at Charity. 'We really must come to some decision.'

'I can't,' Charity told him unhappily. 'Not in so short a time.'

That was during lunch. Gabriel hung about all afternoon, and she knew he wanted to speak to her alone, but she clung resolutely to Frances. She guessed from the look in his eyes that given the chance he would bring all the pressure of physical contact to bear upon her. He hoped by violent lovemaking to break down her resistance, to sweep her off her feet and make her pliant to his will. Partly because she feared he might do just that, and partly from a vague repugnance which she did not wholly understand, she made herself elusive. Exciting as his kisses were, she resented such a use of them.

Miranda returned to the attack in a more direct

manner, coming up to the schoolroom upon the following morning and sending Frances upon an improvised errand. During the child's absence, she told her:

'I favour your marriage with my son because you're a sensible girl and will be a good influence upon him. I've always been afraid he might take up with some extravagant floosie who would dissipate his money. He'll be quite comfortably off, though he won't be exactly rich.'

Charity flushed. She had not given the material side much consideration.

'Thank you for the information,' she said drily, 'but isn't it much more important whether we're really suited and whether we love each other?'

'Oh, love,' Miranda was contemptuous. 'That's only one ingredient in marriage, and not a lasting one. Gabriel is wilful and passionate, and though I didn't altogether approve of his idea of eloping, it would at least have presented Jason with a *fait accompli*. My nephew has high moral principles, he wouldn't have allowed you to live in sin.'

'There was no question of that,' Charity cried, her face flaming. 'What's it all got to do with Mr Ollenshaw, anyway?'

'He's the head of the family,' Miranda spoke repressively. 'But you refused to run away, so now what I suggest is this. As soon as Jason returns, you'll tell him that your mother is ill, or some such fairy tale, and that you must go home at once. Then Gabriel will come down and stay in the vicinity, meet your people, and all that. They will, I'm sure, approve of the match, it's very much to your advantage, Charity. With your father being a clergyman, he can put up the banns, officiate at the wedding . . .'

'Oh, please stop!' Charity interrupted. 'We haven't got nearly as far as that yet.'

Miranda's brows went up. 'My dear,' she drawled, 'you've given me the impression you'd gone even farther. Why are you hanging back now?' Charity made no reply, and she went on briskly: 'Anyway, the situation will be quite impossible when Jason is back again. It would be much better if you went home and Gabriel can come after you and make up your mind for you without interference. It is Jason who is upsetting you, isn't it?'

Charity admitted that it was, but not quite in the manner that Miranda meant, for in a flash of illumination she realised that she did not want to leave Carne at all and she was aching to see its master again. This, she knew, was utter folly. All she was to him was a rather tiresome dependant, who, if Gabriel betrayed her, he would believe had broken all her promises to him.

That she thought was only too probable. Gabriel in his present mood was like having high explosive in the house. It seemed she would have to flee, but she did not want Gabriel to follow her, in the role of her fiancé. Faith and her mother would add their persuasions to his, and she wanted time to test her feelings for him.

'I think perhaps I should go home,' she agreed unwillingly. 'As you say, the position here is becoming rather difficult, but I'd sooner Gabriel didn't come for a while, until I'm sure ...'.

'That you'll have to settle with him,' Miranda cut in, 'but don't you realise you've committed yourself? You can hardly let my son down now.'

Frances returned from her errand and her grandmother withdrew, leaving Charity perturbed. Miranda seemed as set upon this marriage as her son was, but the reasons she gave were not very convincing. Charity had an uneasy suspicion that she was a pawn in a game which she did not understand. As for saying she was committed, she had never definitely said that she would marry Gabriel, though she supposed her actions had implied that she was willing.

She would go home and put her problems to her father. Unworldly, wise and tolerant, he would give her the direction which she sought, and once free of Gabriel's physical influence, she would be able to view him dispassionately and the degree to which she missed him would assist her to decide if she wanted to link her life with his.

As she roamed the Clough that afternoon with Frances, she realised how much she had come to love the country in the short time that she had been there, but that was no added inducement to marry Gabriel, for he was set upon leaving it. She was sorry also to be leaving the child, but it was just possible she might be able to return, if she decided against Gabriel, and he turned his attentions in another direction as he had threatened to do. It seemed an unlikely hope, but it comforted her. The plea of illness at home did not mean that her absence would have to be protracted, though in the present crisis it would seem to be advisable.

As on the previous evening, she did not go downstairs, and as the light was beginning to fade, Gabriel burst into the schoolroom.

'Why are you avoiding me?' he demanded. 'This is our last chance to be together before the Sultan comes home. Don't you love me at all?'

'I . . . I don't know.' Her heart had begun to hammer furiously at the sight of him, but her emotion was mainly fear.

He pulled her out of her chair and into his arms and began to caress her, but she failed to respond. Removing his mouth from hers, he stared broodingly into her pale face, around which her loosened hair hung in heavy waves.

'You aren't going to let me down?' he asked menacingly.

'Oh, Gabriel, I feel all at sea,' she said wearily. 'And Mr Ollenshaw's coming home tomorrow, and I'm sure he'll suspect . . .' Her voice trailed away.

'If you hadn't been such a little idiot we'd have been across the Channel by now,' he reminded her, 'with the bogey-man coming home to find the birds flown. But you've nothing to be afraid of. Just tell him you've got

132

to go home and once you're away from here, you can forget all about him.'

'I suppose so,' she sighed. She hesitated. Should she tell Gabriel that she did not want him to follow her to Maytree, that she did not think she could bring herself to marry him? She looked at him consideringly and his good looks struck her afresh. Lithe, debonair, his dark hair ruffled, his eyes alight with passion, he looked irresistible, and when she had first met him he had epitomised romance, but there was also something diabolical about him, and she remembered that even then he had made her think of Lucifer the fallen angel.

She dreaded the storm which her words would evoke, and doubted her own ability to withstand him. Much better to go home and write to him from there, but here at Carne she felt too vulnerable, and if she sought protection from Jason, the result would be the same. He would send her home in disgrace and it would be more dignified to leave of her own accord without betraying that she had disobeyed him.

'You don't seem very enthusiastic,' he complained. He glanced towards her bedroom door. 'There's one way of clinching the matter, and I'm tired of waiting.'

Shocked, she cried out vehemently: 'No!' Then remembering Frances she dropped her voice. 'We mustn't wake Frances, her door's open.'

'That darned kid's always your refuge,' he said angrily. 'Thank God you'll be leaving her behind.'

A revulsion of feeling swept over Charity with illuminating force. She had never loved Gabriel, he had bewitched her, but now he terrified her.

He said half pityingly: 'You're a sentimental little idiot, Charity. When are you going to face up to the realities of life?' As she made no answer, his face darkened threateningly. 'It seems I'll have to bring them home to you, and if you fail me now, you'll find they can be exceedingly harsh.'

After which cryptic utterance, he wished her a perfunctory goodnight, and left the room.

Charity sat staring into the dusky shadows in the

corners, which seemed to menace her. She must go home at once, she dared no longer stay at Carne.

Jason returned upon the following afternoon. Frances, who was having tea, heard his voice outside and ran to the open window. He was strolling on the lawn with Paula Stevens, wearing a grey suit and looking more like a greyhound than ever. Paula was dressed in a scarlet trouser suit which became her dark prettiness, and she was laughing up into his face. Having joined Frances at the window, Charity heard him say:

'Weren't you a bit rash to lend Gabriel your car?'

'It was insured,' Paula returned. 'And I didn't need it while I was away. I've an idea he wanted to cut a dash with your demure little nannie.'

Aware that she was eavesdropping, Charity drew hurriedly back, while Frances clamoured to be allowed to go down and greet him.

'I don't see why not,' Charity agreed, 'but come straight back if he tells you to.'

She remained in the schoolroom and presently saw Frances speed across the lawn and throw herself upon Jason. He continued his stroll with the child between him and Paula, each holding a hand. Charity watched them with an ache in her heart, remembering that tea at Buxton when Frances had said they were like a family and Jason's comments. May and October seemed to be bridging the age gap, and no one could imagine Paula was Jason's daughter.

He brought Frances back some while later. Charity's heart beat fast at sight of him. His grey suit became him and he was bronzed by the summer sun, his eyes looking almost startlingly blue. He greeted her kindly and then they began to discuss Frances' birthday treat, for that auspicious date would soon be upon them. Frances was all for the Pavilion Gardens, but Jason suggested the caves at Castleton as a more ambitious outing.

'In the Speedwell you go along in a boat,' he told her.

'But is it dark?'

'Oh no, it's all lit by electricity.'

'And Nannie will come too?'

Jason smiled at Charity. 'Of course, and we'll buy her a bit of Blue John, that is a sort of mineral which is found in Castleton, the only place where it's mined in the whole world.'

'I'd treasure it,' she said, but she felt slightly sick. Jason would never buy her a piece of Blue John. When he took Frances to Castleton, she would be far away. He was looking at her with some concern.

'You look pale, Charity. That blow on your head— it's all right now?'

'Oh yes, I've forgotten all about it.'

'You've been indoors too much, perhaps? We'll have a canter on the moors tomorrow morning. That'll bring your colour back.'

Nothing escaped him, and although his solicitude pleased her, she knew it was undeserved.

'Is you coming too?' Frances asked eagerly.

'Yes, for your first outing,' he promised, his eyes lingering on Charity with a questioning look as if he sensed something was wrong.

She clenched her hands. It was not going to be easy to offer a bogus excuse for her departure.

She decided to leave the matter until the next day, when a letter from home was due and would lend colour to her story. The post came late at Carne, so first she would have her ride on the moors. She found that she was looking forward to it with passionate eagerness.

It seemed like a return to a past era to be dressing in her jodhpurs and helping Frances with hers. It was a grey morning, but as they ran out to the stables, the sun pushed its way through the clouds.

It was good to be on a horse again, to feel Lola's powerful stride beneath her, the clean wind in her face and—to have Jason by her side. The magic of the moors, she thought, and a little demon of recklessness entered into her. She urged Lola into a canter, then a gallop, and the exhilarating pace excited her. She could have shouted for joy. When they came to a low stone wall across their path, Lola skimmed over it without unseating her. She became aware of pounding hooves behind her and Jason calling to her to halt. For a few minutes she held her pace, then pulled Lola up and Jason came up alongside of her.

'You're not running a race,' he rebuked her, looking at the mare's heaving sides. Then he laughed. 'You ride like an Amazon. When you took that jump my heart was in my mouth, but you did it perfectly. I'll have to consider you for exhibition purposes. Would you like to ride one of my horses at a show?'

'I'd love to,' she cried, forgetting that she would be leaving.

'Poor Frances,' he observed, looking round. 'We've left her far behind. Her beast's legs are too short to keep up with ours.'

Frances was cantering bravely after them, and they waited side by side for her to catch up with them. Jason looked round appreciatively at the long bare slopes where the ling was turning purple.

'France is a beautiful country,' he said. 'But give me my hills every time.'

'Did Miss Stevens like France?' Charity asked.

'Paula? Oh yes, she went to Paris. I imagine she'd enjoy that. Personally I hate towns. I was in a remote part of Normandy.'

So he had not been with Paula after all. Charity was suddenly elated.

'But you, Charity,' he went on, a worried pucker between his brows, and his eyes kinder than she had ever seen them. 'You've lost your serenity. You always seemed to be so contented. What's troubling you?' Their knees were almost touching and he put out a hand, laying it over hers upon her reins. 'Tell me and I'll see if I can put it right.'

She looked down upon the brown, sinewy hand that felt so warm and comforting through misty eyes. She had a longing to throw herself into his arms, to sob out

136

all her perplexities and confusion against his chest, but she knew that if she told him, his lean face would harden to granite, his eyes become icy.

'There's nothing the matter,' she said flatly.

Frances came up to them, her eyes accusing.

'You runned away and left me,' she reproached them.

'But you've caught us up, riding like a centaur,' Jason told her. 'We won't run away again. Your nannie rather forgot herself.'

Charity smiled wryly. A timely reminder. Nannies did not weep upon their employer's shoulder, and he had again put her in her place. But if ever she married Gabriel that place would be considerably elevated. She glanced at Jason smiling down at Frances, so unconscious of her dilemma. It would serve him right if she did; he had no right to despise her because of her inferior position, but she could no longer whip up indignation against him. She did not believe that he did despise her.

They rode slowly home to let the horses cool off, while Frances chattered volubly. Jason was silent, but from time to time Charity was conscious of his eyes upon her and knew he had not been satisfied with her denial.

Her letter should have come by the time they reached the house, and this afternoon or this evening she would tell him that she must return home. She hoped desperately that he would not be sympathetic; that would be hard to bear, knowing that her excuse was a fabrication. She would prefer that he would be annoyed at the abrupt termination of her engagement, that would show him in a less favourable light, and the last thing she wanted to do was to think well of Jason.

But when they had stabled their horses and he parted with them at the entrance to the house, she was again near to tears. It was unlikely that she would ever gallop again on the magic moors with Jason Ollenshaw.

There was a letter for her lying upon the hall table. She picked it up, noting with surprise that the handwriting was Faith's, not her mother's, and a premonition of trouble smote her. Why had not Mrs Castle written as usual?

Hurriedly she shepherded Frances upstairs and told her to change her clothes, while she slit the envelope with unsteady fingers. Her premonition was correct. Mr Castle had had a stroke and was in hospital, while her mother was staying at the Manor, too upset to write herself.

'There's no sense in you coming home,' her sister wrote. 'The Vicarage is closed and I can't put you up as well as Mother. We'll let you know as soon as there's any change. The doctor is hopeful of ultimate recovery, so there's no need to get into a flap. If he asks for you, we'll have to find somewhere for you to stay, but at present he can't speak and we're in an awful muddle.'

A letter typical of Faith with one thing very clear. She did not want Charity to come back.

Charity was overwhelmed with guilt. The makebelieve excuse had become a grim reality, with the difference that she had no home to go to. In her emotional state it seemed to her that she had wished the stroke upon her father, when she had contemplated pleading illness as a reason for going home, forgetting the idea had originally been Miranda's.

She desperately wanted to go to her father, and since Faith was so unco-operative, she began to mentally review her friends in Maytree, wondering whom she could approach with a request for a bed. She could not allow consideration for Faith's convenience to prevent her from being with her parents in their hour of trial.

She went down to lunch as usual and unable to contain her news, she blurted it out to the assembled family.

'I must go,' she said. 'I mayn't be any use, but I must be there. Please, Mr Ollenshaw, will you release me from my duties? My sister makes light of it, but ... but

'... Daddy might die.' She burst into tears.

Frances immediately climbed down from her chair and ran to her, throwing her arms about her.

'Nannie, Nannie, don't cry ...' and frightened by Charity's tears, she began to sob loudly herself.

Miranda and Gabriel exchanged meaning glances, and in the midst of her distress, Charity realised with a sensation of horror that they thought she was acting. She wanted to cry out that her news was true, a terrible punishment for her duplicity, but no words would come.

It was Jason who took the situation in hand. Gently disengaging Frances' clinging arms, he told her to go to Annie and leave her nannie to him. She needed a rest and would soon be herself again. Then, putting his arm round Charity, he raised her to her feet and led her away to the morning room. Arrived there, he put her into the most comfortable chair and poured out for her his usual panacea, a glass of wine.

'Of course I'll release you,' he told her, 'but you're in no fit state to travel today. I'll take you to the station myself to catch the first train in the morning, that'll give you time to calm down and do your packing. Meanwhile I'll phone the hospital ... do you know which it is?'

She shook her head. Faith had omitted to mention that.

'Mrs Foster is on the phone, isn't she? I'll get in touch with her. Aunt will know the number. I'll tell her how distressed you are and get the latest news. I'll also insist that she makes arrangements for your accommodation.'

He looked down compassionately at her bent brown head. 'Too bad this has happened just when you'd settled down. But you'll come back to us, won't you, Charity, whatever happens?' He had given up all pretence of calling her Miss Castle.

'I don't know,' she said dully. If only she could!

'You must. Frances will be heartbroken if you don't ... and I shall miss you.'

The last phrase was almost inaudible. She raised her head quickly and met his eyes through a mist of tears. They were neither steely nor icy, but infinitely kind, and somewhere in their depths a tiny flame flickered.

'Oh, don't,' she choked. 'I ... can't bear any more.'

'Don't try to talk.'

He bent over her, putting an arm round her shoulders, wiping her eyes with his own clean handkerchief. She caught a whiff of leather, and soft soap mingled with Old Spice.

'Perhaps I should come with you,' he ruminated. 'You don't look fit to travel alone.'

She broke into hysterical laughter. To arrive under Jason's escort when she had been planning to flee from his cousin held an element of farce. As her laughter grew wilder, he slapped her face.

'Stop it!'

She ceased abruptly and he again wiped her eyes.

'I'm sorry, but that was necessary,' he told her. 'I'll go and make that phone call. Just sit here quietly and drink up that wine. It'll do you good. I'll see you're not disturbed.'

He went to the door, took the key out of the lock and went out. She heard the click as he turned it upon the further side.

She sat quite still, slowly recovering her self-control, aware of a deep and glowing content. Jason would see to everything for her, grapple with Faith and defeat her, arrange the details of her journey and obtain the latest news of her father.

It did not occur to her that Gabriel might react unfavourably to Jason's attentiveness. She did not think of him at all.

Jason was as good as his word. After a lengthy conversation with Faith, who became co-operative as soon as she discovered who he was, he obtained not only the name of the hospital but a promise to arrange accommodation for her sister.

The hospital divulged, somewhat unwillingly, the information that Mr Castle's condition was unchanged. He also checked the time of the morning train and repeated his offer to travel with Charity, which she declared was quite unnecessary. She was not an invalid and by the next day the effects of the shock she had sustained would have worn off.

Frances, who had to be told that her nannie was leaving her, was inconsolable. In an effort to comfort her, Charity let her stay up past her usual bedtime and she was modelling half-heartedly with her Plasticine when Miranda and Paula came into the schoolroom. Paula, who had been to tea, was again clad in her red trouser suit, the line of which suggested she had bought it in Paris. Pale and wan in a dark print dress, Charity felt entirely eclipsed by the other girl's slightly flamboyant appearance.

'Good, you're still up,' Miranda said unexpectedly. 'So you can go back with Paula right away,' and as Frances threw her a startled glance, she went on to explain that Paula had asked that the child should spend a few days at Woodlands.

'We've some cousins staying with us,' Paula told them, 'and they've a boy and a girl of about Fran's age. We thought you might like to come and play with them, Frances.'

Frances was delighted. She had all the only child's hankering after others of her kind. While Charity packed some clothes for her, she questioned Paula eagerly about little Alan and Mary, and Charity was grateful to Miss Stevens for providing a diversion for her.

When it came to the actual parting, her kiss and hug were a trifle perfunctory, for her thoughts were already at Woodlands, and she went off in Paula's car full of eager anticipation.

Charity went back upstairs to do her own packing, wondering a little sadly if she would ever see her again.

She had not seen Gabriel to speak to since her collapse at lunch time, and as it was Annie's evening off, dinner downstairs would be a casual meal, so that she felt sure he would find an opportunity to come to her. She dreaded seeing him, but at least she owed him a farewell interview and perhaps he would be kind. If he were in reality her fiancé, he would be the person to whom she should turn in her distress, not his cousin, and if he had any genuine feeling for her at all, he should give her the support and sympathy she needed in greater measure than an employer, however generous.

Jason had been more than kind, but it was Gabriel who sought a closer relationship with her. If his reaction to her bad news was as sympathetic as it should be, it would do much to mitigate the fear and revulsion which she had begun to feel towards him.

Mrs Appleton came to remove her supper tray and stayed to offer condolences, which were interspersed with accounts of her own relations who had made miraculous recoveries from strokes. Finally, to Charity's relief, she took her leave.

A few minutes later Gabriel tapped upon the door.

'Come in,' Charity called, guessing it was he. He entered with a confident, triumphant look which caused her a flutter of apprehension. Instinctively she retreated to the window, putting the table between them, but Gabriel was too elated to notice the significance of her action.

'Congratulations,' he said cheerfully. 'It all went off splendidly, but was it necessary to cause quite such a commotion? I saw red when Jason took it upon himself to act as wet nurse to you. Do you know, he actually locked you up and refused to let me come near you?'

Apparently he still thought that she had been acting, but it would have taken a great actress to feign the anguish she had felt.

'One might almost imagine the ninny was in love with you himself,' he went on. 'Does he think he's a right to every girl on the place? Sort of *droit du seigneur*.' He laughed. 'But you rather overdid the waterworks, didn't you, love?'

He looked at her with mock reproach across the table, upon which were some of Frances' efforts at modelling, barely recognisable shapes of horses and dogs.

Since it was a warm evening, he wore only a silk shirt and dark trousers, having discarded his jacket after dinner, and he fairly glowed with health and vitality, which, since she felt drained and washed out, seemed to Charity almost an affront, but not more so than his ill-chosen words.

'But, Gabriel,' she protested, 'I wasn't acting. My father really has had a stroke.'

He laughed again. 'How very convenient of him! It made your performance so completely convincing.'

This egotistical utterance roused her to near fury. She leaned across the table towards him, her eyes flashing. 'Don't you understand, my father is dangerously ill. How can you be so callous?'

He looked at her in surprise. 'You mean you really care about him?'

'Of course I do.'

'No of course at all. I hated my father. Perhaps that's going to complicate matters a bit?'

Charity drew back with a movement of swift recoil. Filial affection apparently had no place in Gabriel's life. Even if he had not got on with his father, he showed his doting mother scant consideration. In an intuitive flash, she realised that he was incapable of caring for anyone except himself and could not really love her. Nevertheless she tried to reason with him.

'Gabriel, I love my father,' she told him earnestly. 'Until I know he's going to recover, I can't think about anything else.'

'And when will you know that?'

'I've no idea. I ... we ... will just have to wait and try to endure the suspense.'

'And while you're enduring it, I'm expected to hang about indefinitely? It's not good enough, and it's not fair to me.'

He had failed her utterly. All that concerned him

was what he saw as a hitch to his own plans, plans in which she would never now consent to participate. All she wanted to do was to get rid of him as quickly as possible, and without causing an unpleasant scene, which she felt unequal to facing.

'I'm leaving tomorrow morning,' she said quietly. 'I'll write to you from Maytree and let you know what is happening. It would help me so much if you would try to understand . . .'

'I can't understand such a fuss about a mere parent,' he interrupted, beginning to scowl. 'I thought everything was working out nicely, but it seems to me that you're ready to jump at any excuse to put me off.'

His eyes were beginning to glow ominously and his brows contract over them, but she faced him bravely.

'I've had a shock, Gabriel, I can only think that . . . that Daddy might die.' Her voice broke.

'You're a sentimental little idiot,' he returned angrily. 'I refuse to take second place to a mere father. You're going to marry me, Charity, and soon. My patience is exhausted.'

He came at her then, sweeping her into his arms in an embrace that was full of fury and held nothing of love. She was limp in his hold, vainly trying to turn her face away from his demanding lips. Neither of them heard the door open.

'Stop that, Gabriel!'

It was Jason's voice, low-pitched but with the quality of steel. Gabriel released Charity abruptly and stood sullenly regarding his cousin, while Charity covered her face with her hands to conceal her confusion. She would have given anything not to be caught by him in Gabriel's arms.

Jason looked from one to the other.

'May I have an explanation?' he asked coldly.

'Certainly,' Gabriel was nonchalant. 'Charity and I are going to get married, so there's no need for you to butt in.'

'Indeed?' He looked at Charity. 'Is this true?' he asked her.

Dumbly she shook her head, and Gabriel rounded on her.

'What do you mean by that? You love me, don't you?'

'God pity you if you do,' Jason said coldly.

'You can keep your pity,' Gabriel flung at him. 'Charity is doing a good thing for herself by marrying me. You did your best to keep us apart, but you might have known it would happen.'

'I'm sorry,' Charity said gently. 'It must look to you as if I've broken all my promises, but it wasn't altogether my fault. You see, even nannies have feelings.' She wanted to make him understand that she was a woman with a woman's heart, not a mere employee. 'And one can't always control one's emotions.' She drew herself up proudly. 'Though I may be poor and insignificant, that's no reason why I shouldn't make a good wife.'

She threw the words at him, like a challenge, nor did she look insignificant as she uttered them, with her eyes dark with intensity, and a wild rose flush in her cheeks.

'I don't doubt it,' he said, to her amazement. His glance moved towards his cousin and his face darkened. 'The question is, will Gabriel make you a good husband?'

'You've always had your knife into me,' the other man told him angrily. 'Just because I'm not staid and stodgy like Martin is, but ...' a mocking look came into his eyes, 'a good wife might redeem me.'

Jason tilted his chair backwards, thrusting his hands into his trouser pockets while he regarded Gabriel coldly.

'I rather think you're past redemption,' he remarked. 'Does Charity know why you're so anxious to rush into matrimony?'

'Oh, that,' Gabriel exclaimed carelessly. 'I don't suppose it would make much difference to her now she's got to know me.' He turned to Charity with an insolent air. 'What Jason doubts is the genuineness of my attachment to you,' he told her. 'But before we discuss that, I'd better tell you, since if I don't, he will, certain facts. My late father left a considerable amount of money to be divided between his sons, but he had an addlepated notion that if he happened to die prematurely, which in fact he did, a large sum of money might present temptation to a young man. He believed, you see, in the virtue of working for a living, so, except for a small income paid out of interest upon capital, we were not to enjoy the bulk of his estate until we'd reached thirty years of age, or married in the meantime. He also believed apparently in the stabilising influence of marriage.' He shot Jason a barbed look. 'Well, the old man died,' he continued, 'while we were still at school. Martin went into business, did well, married young and in due course received his share and did even better. I'm not married and am only twenty-six—four more years to go before I can get my hands on all that lovely lolly, unless you take pity on me, as I'm sure you will.'

He held himself jauntily, still confident that he could bend her to his will in spite of his disclosure.

Jason said harshly: 'He's incapable of appreciating you, Charity, and once he has obtained his money, he'll proceed to break your heart.'

'Oh, come off it,' Gabriel protested. 'I don't think Charity's heart is quite the fragile organ you imagine, dear Jason, and she's also got a head on her shoulders.'

'I have,' Charity told him meaningly, 'and it doesn't seem to me that hearts have anything to do with your calculations.' She was beginning to understand all that had puzzled her—Gabriel's insistence upon an early marriage, his alternate moods of advance and retreat. Even with such a gilded goal ahead, he had had difficulty in reconciling himself to such a plain and naïve mate.

'It would have saved a lot of misunderstanding if I'd been told the real situation from the beginning,' she went on coolly. 'Then there would have been no need for your amorous act, Gabriel, nor ...' Her eyes turned

146

to Jason. 'Your veiled warnings and tyrannous behaviour.'

'I'm sorry you found me a tyrant,' Jason returned equally coolly, 'but you did assure me you wouldn't let yourself become involved, and I hoped it would not be necessary to enlighten you.'

'Family loyalty and all that?' Gabriel jeered. 'You thought you'd only got to tell Charity to be a good girl and she would obey you blindly, but she isn't quite such a fool as all that.'

He turned to Charity, wiping the mockery from his face, and he spoke sincerely:

'Of course I wanted a wife—who wouldn't under the circumstances? I told you more than once how much I need you, but I didn't tell you why because you're such a romantic twit you'd have been revolted to think I wanted to marry you for my money, but I meant to let you share in my riches while they lasted, and I fully intended to fulfil all my husbandly duties, you can be sure of that.'

Charity flinched and Gabriel laughed merrily at her expression.

'In fact I was looking forward to initiating you,' he added with a hint of brutality. Jason made a movement of distaste.

'Skip it!' he said sharply.

'Oh, very well,' Gabriel shrugged. 'But my offer is still open, Charity. As Jason has kindly pointed out, I may not make an ideal husband, but you're not likely to have a better offer. I promise I'll give you some fun, and regarding the love business that you're so intrigued about, perhaps I can scrape up something that will satisfy you. There are other emotions which provide quite a good substitute. Anyway, who believes in deathless love nowadays?'

'We know you don't,' Jason said acidly. He hesitated, then went on quickly, 'Charity, I don't suppose Gabriel has mentioned Samantha Davis, and why he came to Carne?'

Gabriel flushed darkly. 'No!' he exclaimed violently. 'Why should she know? It's all past history. My licence has been renewed and you're no longer responsible for my good behaviour.'

'But your temper's no better,' Jason pointed out, 'and that demon is something Charity would have to live with.'

'It was Sam's fault,' Gabriel declared. 'She threatened to break off our engagement if I didn't mend my ways.'

He caught Charity's look. She had not thought of that.

'Oh yes, Charity, I've been engaged before. You don't suppose I'd have waited until now to try to find a wife? But Sam was crippled ...' He flashed an angry glance at Jason. 'It was an accident, the other fellow ran into us. Sam was a fool, only an idiot would jilt a man while he's driving a car. You all talked as if I'd meant to kill her, but I only wanted to frighten her a little. It was just bad luck we met something on a bend.'

Jason said coldly: 'The magistrate didn't take that view. I sometimes think that filthy temper of yours is pathological. However, you escaped with a suspended licence and a heavy fine, which I paid for you on condition you came here and made yourself useful. But that wasn't all. When you thought Samantha was crippled for life, you deserted her.'

'She'd already tried to jilt me,' Gabriel pointed out, 'and I ask you'—he seemed genuinely surprised—'am I the sort of man who could devote himself to an invalid wife? Even to get my money that was expecting a bit too much. I'm not a monk. I should only have been unfaithful to her.'

'You've a point there,' Jason agreed.

'Of course you're a plaster saint,' Gabriel said rudely. 'But I'm a man. I thought I'd find plenty of other girls available here at Carne, but the only presentable one preferred you until Charity came along.'

'This girl,' Charity asked faintly. 'Is she still a cripple?'

148

'No. Luckily she recovered after all,' Jason told her.

Gabriel gaped at him. 'How do you know that?'

Jason shrugged his shoulders. 'I thought it was only right to keep in touch with her to show her someone in the family wasn't indifferent to her fate.'

He would think of that, Charity decided, but his altruism depressed her. The kindnesses he had shown her had nothing personal about them, they were merely his natural bent.

'I suppose you sent her flowers and held her hand,' Gabriel was jeering. 'I'm surprised you didn't feel called upon to console her by marrying her yourself.'

'She didn't want me,' Jason said. 'Strangely enough she was still in love with you. I don't suppose you've any inkling of what that poor girl went through, knowing what you were, your selfishness and temper, your roving propensities, while her common sense battled with her love. She only threatened to give you up in the hope that you would try to improve.' He moved restlessly. 'I don't want to see Charity in a similar predicament.'

'So that's what all this has been leading up to?' Gabriel asked scornfully. 'Did Charity also unbosom herself to you in the sanctuary of the morning room?' He looked at her suspiciously. 'Am I to blame because girls foolishly fall in love with me?'

'Then why did you select me for your attentions?' Charity asked. 'I should have thought I was the last person to appeal to you.'

'You happened to be handy,' Gabriel returned coolly. 'Actually you were my mother's choice in the first place. She saw you at that place in Essex, decided you were suitable and brought you up here like a lamb to the slaughter. It saved me the trouble of going further afield, and you were so susceptible.'

'Don't mock me,' she said, flushing painfully.

'But I'm not mocking you, love. You know you always intrigued me. You seemed too good to be true in these modern times.'

'She's too good for you,' Jason interposed. 'Perhaps

you'll understand now, Charity, why I wanted you to steer clear of Gabriel. What you do about him is not my affair, but at least you've been warned.'

She had suspected for some time that there was some motive behind the Dalrymples' eagerness to hurry on this marriage, but she wished it had not had to be revealed in Jason's presence. It humiliated her.

Gabriel was standing frowning blackly, then suddenly his face cleared, and he smiled at her sunnily.

'As I said, a good wife will redeem me,' he said confidently. 'That's what Miranda hoped when she brought you here, and she also hoped Jason wouldn't notice how guileless and innocent you were.'

He came nearer to her, regarding her with the sleepy, sensuous look which she had always found so devastating.

'Jason's finished his indictment,' he told her. 'There are no more awful revelations, and he's tried to show me in the worst possible light, and I didn't really mean to harm that poor girl. Perhaps it has come as a shock to your romantic susceptibilities to discover I'm not in love with you, but I daresay our marriage will work out all right, and you realise now why it must be soon. So you won't let me down, will you, love? I've waited long enough for that money ...' He paused and looked intently at her bowed head. 'Well, what are you going to do about it?' he asked impatiently.

It was very still in the schoolroom. Out of doors a little wind had risen and moaned softly round the house, and when an owl screeched, the ill-omened cry sounded unnaturally loud in the silence.

Gabriel moved restlessly. 'Well?' he demanded sharply. 'What have you decided?'

The emergency with which Charity was faced had temporarily been driven from her mind during the clash between the two men, but now it returned to her with added force.

'I can't decide anything now,' she cried wildly. 'I can only think of Daddy,' and she buried her face in her hands.

Gabriel smothered an imprecation and Jason rose to his feet.

'Out you go, Gabriel,' he commanded. 'Charity needs a good night's sleep. When she knows how her father is going to be, she'll get in touch with you and give you her answer. Isn't that so, Charity?'

'Yes,' she agreed, thankful for the respite. 'I can't think straight now.'

She looked beseechingly at Gabriel, seeking some understanding in his face. Had he shown kindness then, some sympathy for her anxiety, she might have softened towards him, for it seemed he needed her, while Jason did not, but all his features expressed was a furious impatience.

'You're not to bother her any more tonight,' Jason said sternly.

Gabriel took a step towards her, then meeting Jason's steely look, moved towards the door.

'Goodnight, Charity,' he said over his shoulder. '*Au'voir* until we meet again.' The black eyes had an evil glitter.

As soon as the door had closed behind him, Jason came over to her.

'For God's sake give him up,' he urged her. 'There's no need to walk into hell out of a mistaken sense of loyalty, and life with him would be hell, I can assure you.'

She said nothing and her eyelids drooped.

'You've had enough for one day,' he said kindly. 'Go to bed and sleep.'

He waited until she had gone into her bedroom, and as she closed the door, she saw he was still watching her with an inscrutable expression in his eyes.

CHAPTER SEVEN

CHARITY could not sleep. The day had produced too many shocks. Her father's illness, the revelations about Gabriel, the sorry tangle of her relations with him, which she knew now was nothing but a foolish involvement, the stronger emotion she was beginning to feel towards the master of Carne, an emotion which could bring her nothing but pain, were like so many rats gnawing at her tired brain. At least she had another valid excuse for leaving Carne, and she could never return as long as Gabriel was there.

At length in the early hours, she fell into a fitful doze, only to be brought wide awake by a crash of thunder overhead. Her hand went to her bedside lamp without result; the electricity was off. A brilliant violet flare lit the room and the thunder boomed and reverberated among the hills.

Charity jumped out of bed, reaching for her dressing gown, with the intention of going to Frances, then remembered that Frances was at Woodlands.

She fumbled her way to the window, but outside it was pitch dark until the lightning flashed, showing a wild scene of tossing trees and racing cloud. The storm was directly overhead.

In the next flash, she found her torch and made her way into the schoolroom, wondering if anyone else was up, as it was unlikely that anybody could sleep through the racket. She wanted the assurance of another human presence; she did not care for bad thunderstorms.

Noiselessly she opened the schoolroom door and looked out into the black tunnel of the passage. Lightning again flickered and Charity saw there was someone there, and with dismay recognised Gabriel.

She flicked off her torch and stepped back into the shelter of the schoolroom, but not quickly enough; he sprang forward before she could shut the door and put his foot in it.

'Don't run away,' he said softly. 'It's a shocking storm, isn't it?'

'Yes, I was a bit scared,' she admitted. 'I was wondering if anyone else was up.'

The lightning flickered almost continuously, and she could see he was still fully dressed, but she had on only a thin dressing gown and her hair was loose over her shoulders. In the uncertain illumination, he was a dark menacing presence looming over her.

'As you see, I am,' he pointed out. 'Jason is too—he's gone out to the stables to make sure the gee-gees are all right.'

Charity stood in the doorway, unwilling to retreat in case he followed her. She did not want to be shut in the schoolroom alone with him.

He said silkily: 'Perhaps the storm gave you an excuse to come to look for me?'

'No,' she returned quickly. 'I told you, I was just scared.'

'What a pity, seeing that it's your last night under the same roof with me.' His tone was mocking. 'Come off it, Charity, you aren't really going to ditch me, are you?'

She drew a deep breath and then said firmly:

'You may as well have it straight. I'm sorry, but I can't marry you, it was all a mistake.'

In the tense pause that followed, the lightning flashed, illuminating the corridor from end to end, each of its uncurtained windows a golden oblong. In its glare she saw Gabriel's face. It looked like that of a devil.

'So you've been playing with me, have you?' he accused. 'And now the master has returned, you think he's a better proposition. Is that it?' He felt for her wrist and seized it. 'Is it?'

'No!' she cried, trying to free herself. 'That's quite untrue, and you know he only cares for Paula.'

'Oh yes? And that's why he locked you in the morning room so I couldn't come near you? You're a deep one, Charity, deeper than I gave you credit for. God, I've a good mind to wring your scheming little neck!'

Charity became terrified; she well knew Gabriel's violent temper and he held her wrist in a grip of steel. Another blaze lit the passage as she struggled to break away from him. Then to her intense relief a wavering light came towards them from the head of the stairs and they were no longer alone. The light from a powerful torch was shone on the couple in the doorway and from behind it came Jason's stern voice:

'Gabriel, I told you to leave Miss Castle alone!'

'But she didn't want to be left alone,' Gabriel said suavely. 'She's frightened of the storm. I happened to be passing and I was trying to reassure her.'

He had dropped Charity's wrist and she rubbed it mechanically. It felt as if it were broken.

'Well, I'm here now,' Jason observed coolly. 'So you can go to bed.'

'Oh, I can, can I?' Gabriel's voice was low and furious. 'I've known all along you wanted her yourself, for all your pious humbug. That's the real reason for your tale-bearing, sneak! No doubt she'd suit you very well, she's as prim as you are, but I happen to have first claim ...'

'Shut up,' Jason interrupted. 'Get to bed, and since I can do no more for you, I should be obliged if you removed yourself from Carne altogether. The place will be a lot pleasanter without you.'

Gabriel raised his fists and took a step towards his cousin, but something in the older man's face restrained him, and he paused uncertainly

'I shouldn't if I were you,' Jason warned him.

Gabriel lowered his hands and swore. 'Oh, very well,' he said sulkily. 'But you're a spoil-sport, Jason, intruding upon our last night together.' His dark eyes glittered. 'I wish you joy of my leavings!'

With which parting shot he was gone, a black shadow against the intermittent flickerings at the windows, and Charity gave a sigh of relief as he disappeared.

She stepped back into the schoolroom, wondering if

Jason could possibly credit Gabriel's insinuations. In her perturbation, and the uncertain gleam from her torch, she knocked herself sharply against a piece of furniture. The acute pain caused her to give a stifled sob.

Jason put his own torch down on the table and took her into his arms, as gently as if she had been a scared child. She clung to him, all the pent-up emotions and tensions of the day breaking in a storm of weeping. He held her closely, stroking her head soothingly without speaking. Gabriel had been a sinister shadow, but Jason was consolation in the enfolding dark.

The storm was passing away, the thunder becoming a distant growl, the lightning a wan flicker against the first light breaking in the east. Outside the rain was falling in a steady torrent.

Charity's tears ceased, but she was reluctant to withdraw from the shelter of Jason's encircling arms. It was sheer heaven to be held by him and receive, if not the love she craved, his solicitude. Finally it was he who put her from him.

'Let's have a little light on the scene,' he suggested. 'There should be a candle somewhere. We always keep them handy for emergencies.'

He shone the torch round the room while Charity sought and found a box of tissues and wiped her face.

There were two red candles on the mantelpiece in brass sticks, relics of a bygone Christmas. Jason lit them from matches he carried in his pocket. The illumination seemed startlingly bright after the gloom, though it was in fact subdued. He crossed to the window and drew the heavy curtains against the pattering rain.

'That's cosier,' he remarked cheerfully, and turned to survey her. 'Feeling better?'

'Much better,' she said with faint embarrassment, for now he was an identity again and no longer a nebulous comforter in the dark. 'Oh, what you must think of me?' she burst out. 'Crying like a kid.'

'You were frightened,' he reminded her, and she

knew it was not only the storm to which he referred. 'Yes, come in?' For there was a tentative knock on the door.

It opened to reveal Mrs Appleton carrying a lighted candle, a weird figure in her *déshabillé*, for her scanty grey hair was in two tiny pigtails, and she wore a blanket wrapped about her shoulders over her voluminous nightgown, her feet being encased in men's carpet slippers.

She stared in surprise at the sight of her master, who was presenting a far from immaculate appearance. He had gone downstairs in pyjamas and dressing gown, pulling on gumboots and mackintosh in the hall, and though he had discarded these outer garments upon re-entry, his black silk robe was streaked with mud, and pieces of hay were clinging to it.

'I saw t'light. I came to see if summat was oop,' the old woman explained.

Jason told her how Charity had felt nervous and he had found her in the passage upon his return from the stables. He did not mention Gabriel.

'Ay, t'was a rare old tempest,' Mrs Appleton agreed. 'I got oop ma'self to see all t'windows were shut.'

'Since you are up, do you think you could make us a cup of tea?' Jason suggested coaxingly.

'Reckon I could and all. I've a pot brewed, t'missis wanted a coop. I've bin with her.'

So Miranda also was awake, and Charity was glad that she had stayed in her room.

Mrs Appleton shuffled away, and Jason told Charity that they might as well sit down while they waited for the tea. She settled herself in her usual armchair, pulling her dressing gown carefully over her knees, while Jason leaned against the mantelshelf. He produced cigarettes from his dressing gown pocket and lit one from the candle. Charity looked anxiously at his lean, brown face, feeling she must deny Gabriel's nasty innuendoes.

'It wasn't true ... what Gabriel said,' she faltered. 'I ... I've never been with him ...' She flushed crimson with embarrassment.

'You needn't tell me that,' he returned, his eyes on the candle flame. 'Gabriel will say anything when he's angry.'

She remembered the other things that Gabriel had said, and nervously pleated the skirt of her robe, but Jason made no allusion to them. She saw that his hair was ruffled with bits of hay sticking in it, making him look oddly boyish, and involuntarily, she smiled.

'What's the joke?'

'There isn't one, only it's the first time I've ever seen you with a hair out of place.'

He ran his hand over his head and smiled back at her.

'It's the second time I've seen you with your hair down.' He moved from the mantelpiece and drew up a chair beside her. Tentatively he touched one of her long locks. 'You've beautiful hair, Charity.'

'Thank you,' she said simply. She was glad to find there was something about her which pleased him.

'You mustn't get up to catch the early train,' he told her. 'You've had hardly any sleep. If I run you down to Crewe to catch a fast one in the afternoon you won't be much later, and I'll ring the hospital in the morning for news.'

'You're very kind, but what about yourself? You haven't had any sleep either.'

'I'll get a nap before my morning ride. I don't need much sleep.'

They sat in companionable silence, the candles two golden spears in the sombre shadows of the room. Charity was overwhelmingly grateful to the storm for the unexpected bonus of these precious moments of shared intimacy. At length she asked tentatively about the horses.

'They were quite all right, but sometimes they panic when it's very bad. I had to make sure all was well.'

She looked at him out of the corners of her eyes. His face was quiet and grave, his eyes still on her hair. If only there had been a grain of truth in Gabriel's jealous assertions, but she knew his kindness was quite impersonal. It was such a waste that he had never married; he would have made an excellent husband and father.

'What are you thinking of?' he asked. 'You seem very solemn.'

'You'd consider it cheek if I told you,' she returned daringly.

He smiled. 'Try me.'

'Well, actually, I was wondering why you'd never got married.'

He laughed. 'It would be asking a lot of any girl to spend her life at Carne.'

'But it's such a lovely place,' she exclaimed impulsively.

'Do you think so?' He gave her an enigmatical glance. 'But then you've only been here a short while. The winters are very long and dreary, as you'd find out if you had to live here always.'

'I'm sure I shouldn't find them so,' she began, when an awful thought struck her. Gabriel had insinuated in Jason's hearing that she was out to capture him, and he could easily construe her genuine appreciation of Carne to mean she was trying to gain his favour. She went on hastily:

'I daresay you're right, I might get fed up with it after a year or so, and I certainly don't enjoy its thunderstorms.'

'You can get bad storms anywhere,' he pointed out. 'But the youngsters of today are so restless.' He gave a sharp sigh, and she wondered if he were thinking of Paula.

'What will happen to it when ... when you're gone?' she asked, thinking the Dalrymple twins had little interest in the place.

'It'll disintegrate,' he said sadly, 'like most of the old estates. They belong to a past era. That's another reason why I haven't married—there doesn't seem much point in trying to perpetuate a way of life that's already obsolete, and I like the old ways. My cousin considers I'm feudal.' He smiled. 'Feudalism still finds an echo in the Dales, but the echo becomes fainter every year. If I had a son, he'd consider me an antique and want to live somewhere else.'

'Not necessarily,' she protested. 'Not if he loved horses, and surely he would?'

'No guarantee whatever, he'd probably prefer motor-bikes. So to avoid disappointment, Carne and I will pass away together.'

'Aren't you being pessimistic?' Charity was beginning, her whole being revolting from an attitude which seemed to her to be defeatist and barred any woman from the chance to prove him wrong, when the entrance of Mrs Appleton with the tea tray cut short their *tête-à-tête*.

Jason sprang up to move a small table in front of Charity.

'You haven't brought a cup for yourself,' he said as the old woman unloaded her tray, which included a plate of biscuits.

'I had a drop in t'kitchen.'

'Don't tell me you can't manage another one?' Jason's eyes twinkled.

'I don't mind if I do.'

Charity remembered there were beakers in the schoolroom cupboard kept there for Frances' use, who often wanted a drink of some sort. Jason fetched one and resumed his chair beside her. Mrs Appleton seated herself opposite to them, asking Charity to pour out.

It was an odd tea party—the young girl, the master of Carne and the old retainer in their night gear seated at the table by the light of the flickering candles in the early hours of the morning, and in spite of her anxiety about her father, Charity knew an intense happiness. She had never before felt so close to Jason.

Mrs Appleton became expansive about past storms that she had experienced at Carne, but Charity barely listened to her measured tones.

All too soon for her this intimate time in the presence of Jason had to end. Mrs Appleton stood up and started to put the tea-things back on to the tray.

'Happen tha'll sleep the noo,' she said to Charity.

'We'll all sleep,' Jason announced, smothering a yawn. He went to open the door for the old woman. The passage beyond was filled with the wan light of the early summer dawn.

'Jason,' Charity called softly, inadvertently using his name. He came back to her.

'Well?'

'I'd like you to know—I'm not marrying Gabriel,' she said, her eyes on the floor. 'I . . . I couldn't.'

'Thank God for that!' he said fervently. He was standing very close to her, and he stooped and lightly kissed her cheek. 'Sleep well, my child,' he bade her softly.

She went into her bedroom, putting the tips of her fingers on the spot where his lips had touched her, as if by so doing she could retain the brief contact. Those last two words had spoilt it all. He regarded her as a child, another Frances, who needed to be soothed and petted, with no conception that she had become a woman.

Exhausted, Charity slept until late in the morning. She awoke to the realisation that the sun was streaming in through the chinks in the curtains and automatically she glanced at her alarm clock, and saw, since it ran on electricity, that it had stopped.

She got up and went to look at her watch upon the dressing table and saw it was nearly lunch time. Hastily she bathed, dressed and stripped her bed, wondering where she could find Jason without encountering Gabriel. She hoped she could get away without seeing him at all.

She went into the schoolroom, and saw Annie had tidied it. There was no reminder of the midnight tea party except the half burnt candles, and then Miranda came into the room.

'So you're up at last,' she said coldly. 'Gabriel's gone. Took himself off after breakfast without saying where he's going.' A spasm crossed the austere face; what love

160

she was capable of Miranda lavished upon her younger son. 'Heaven knows what will become of him.'

'I'm sorry,' Charity said inadequately, trying to disguise the relief which flooded her at this news.

'So you should be,' Miranda reproved her. 'It was your doing, wasn't it? There was a row last night?'

'Hardly that,' Charity chose her words carefully. 'We were all a little upset by the storm.'

'Jason broke your engagement?'

'We weren't engaged,' Charity corrected her.

'I suppose he put you against my son,' Miranda went on without heeding her objection. 'I know Gabriel's been a little wild, what young man of spirit isn't? But he'd have settled down with you if that interfering nephew of mine had minded his own business.'

Charity put her hand over her wrist, upon which was a circular purple bruise. 'Yes, well ... no doubt he'll find someone more suitable,' she said vaguely. 'Now if you'll excuse me, I must discover if Mr Ollenshaw has any further news about my father.'

'Dutiful daughter, aren't you?' Miranda sneered. 'And Jason is clucking round you like an old hen. I suppose his attentions have turned your head, but if you threw over Gabriel on his account, you'll soon find out your mistake. He'd never consider marrying you.'

There was just enough truth in this remark to cause Charity's face to flame.

'I never dreamed of such a thing,' she cried, 'and Mr Ollenshaw wouldn't ... Oh, what's the use?' she broke off. Miranda was too upset to listen to reason and she must forgive her spiteful words, for she was grieving for her son. 'Since I'm going home I shan't trouble any of you any more,' she concluded quietly.

Jason had rung the hospital again and had better news for her. Mr Castle had recovered consciousness, though he could not speak yet.

'You must eat,' he said, 'then, as I said, I'll drive you down to Crewe. You'll get the London train from there and I've arranged with Mrs Foster for a car to meet you at the other end. We worked out the connection you'll be able to catch at Liverpool Street.'

He had thought of everything for her comfort and he must have spent a fortune in telephone calls.

'I don't know why you should do so much for me,' Charity said impulsively.

'Don't you?' he asked, smiling. 'You've done your best for us, and it's up to us to help you all we can,' he pointed out formally. 'Now you must hurry up if we're to catch that train.'

She tried to eat something of the meal which Mrs Appleton had prepared for her and sent up to the schoolroom. It looked very quiet and peaceful with sunlight pouring into it, yet there she had experienced some of the most dramatic moments of her life.

Not the least of these was the night of the storm, and she threw a last wistful glance round the room before she left it, thinking of how close Jason had seemed upon that occasion.

Mrs Dalrymple was not visible when Charity came downstairs and she thought she would be wise not to seek her out.

Pat brought down her cases and both Mrs Appleton and Annie came into the hall to say goodbye. Mrs Appleton shook her hand, saying:

'I'm reet grieved tha hast to go, lass.'

Annie wished her a pleasant journey.

Standing with her cases beside her outside the front door, waiting for Jason to bring the car round, Charity remembered vividly her arrival only a few months ago. Then it had been Gabriel who had come to greet her and she had been devastated by his good looks. She felt infinitely older and wiser than the awestruck girl who had arrived at Carne upon that chilly spring evening.

Her eyes went to the field where she had watched Jason riding Prince upon her first morning. She had had no premonition then of how her feelings would change towards him. From being a despotic employer he had become the man she loved, and loved without hope of requitement. Nor had she dreamed that Carne would come to be like a second home. She loved every stick and stone of the old grey house and its terraced garden, and to leave it and its owner was proving a wrench that seemed to tear her in two. Even her anxiety to reach her father could not stifle the pain of parting.

The car came down the drive from the stables and Jason got out to open the near side door for her, then proceeded to put her cases in the boot. He was wearing the same grey suit he had worn when he had returned from France, and was as usual perfectly groomed, his hair like a smooth brown cap. Remembering how she had seen it ruffled on the previous night, Charity's lips curved in a little tender smile.

'You seem to have a lot of luggage,' he said, as he entered the seat beside her. 'Couldn't you have left some of your heavier things behind?'

'I didn't want you to have the trouble of sending them after me if I didn't return,' she told him, with a sigh.

The car glided out of the drive and she glanced back to catch a final glimpse of the house through the rear window.

'But you must come back,' he insisted. 'We can't do without you.'

Her face flushed. Could he mean that he had some regard for her after all?

'Poor Fran will be lost without you,' he went on.

The glow was succeeded by a chill. He was only thinking of the child.

'It was very good of Paula—I mean Miss Stevens—to step into the breach,' she said. 'Perhaps she'll continue to console her.'

'I'm afraid Paula had too many other things on her plate,' he observed drily. 'Nor has she much time for children.'

'It'll be different when she has some of her own,' Charity suggested tentatively, glancing at him to see how he reacted to the idea of Paula's possible progeny. Jason shrugged his shoulders.

'Let's hope so,' he said, and began to talk about his

trip to France. Monsieur Briand was hoping to breed a racing winner with Rajah's help, and it was obvious that the horse's possible sons interested Jason much more than Paula's.

The hills gradually faded into the distance as the car crossed the flat Cheshire plain, and they arrived at the railway junction with only a short time to spare, but enough to buy Charity's ticket and an armful of magazines.

The train, the Scottish Express, slid into the crowded platform; it would not stop again until it reached the London terminus and Charity was glad there had not been a wait. It would have been too much to bear.

'There's a buffet car behind if you want coffee or anything,' Jason told her. 'Take care of yourself, and I hope you find your father much better.'

She lowered the window and leaned out. 'Thank you for everything.'

'It's nothing,' he smiled. 'Come back soon.'

The train began to move and he turned away, walking quickly through the thinning crowd on the platform. Charity remained at the window to obtain a last glimpse of the spare, lithe figure, but he did not look back.

It was only too obvious that he had treated her with solicitude to ease the guilt he felt for allowing her to stay at Carne against his better judgment, and it was only for Frances' sake that he wanted her to come back.

CHAPTER EIGHT

RATHER to Charity's surprise, Faith came to meet her at the station herself, driving her own car.

'Mother's gone back to the Vicarage,' she informed her. 'Hope's turned up unexpectedly—seems she's a lot fonder of the old man than she ever let on, so with both of you home, it was the best thing to do. You've heard the latest news about Father? Goodness me, what a fussy old soul your employer is! Seemed to think you weren't capable of finding your own way back. Did you have to buy up the bookstall? Bit unnecessary, wasn't it?

'It was a long journey,' Charity reminded her. She looked out of the car window at the fields of corn coming into ear, and thought wistfully of Carne.

'Did you succeed in making any impression upon Mr Dalrymple?' Faith went on, glancing dubiously at her sister. Tired and strained, Charity was not looking her best. 'I don't suppose you had any luck,' she concluded gloomily.

Charity turned her head away. 'None whatever,' she said.

'Well, it was a bit optimistic to expect he'd take up with a mouse like you,' Faith was scornful, 'and now Hope's turned up looking as if she slept in a haystack. What I've done to deserve two such impossible sisters, I can't imagine!'

Charity merely laughed. What, she wondered, would Faith say if she told her the whole story? That she had been an utter fool. Faith would not have hesitated to take Gabriel upon any terms, but she would have found the devil in him a rather different proposition from the complacent Owen Foster.

Mr Castle recovered rapidly, but he would have to take great care of himself in future; a second stroke

165

might be fatal. Charity spent her life between the hospital and the Vicarage, and later, when he was sent home, nursing her father. He was pathetically grateful for her ministrations, and seemed gratified to have his family around him. Hope was more a hindrance than help, refusing to assist with the chores, and strewing the house with her possessions. Charity was thankful when she finally announced that the country was impossible and took herself and her overworked transistor back to London.

The long summer days slid past in quick succession. Jason had written a formal note enclosing Charity's salary cheque, and she had as formally answered it. Beyond that there had been no further communication with Carne, but her thoughts continually strayed northwards, wondering how Frances—and Jason—were faring. She hoped Faith might have some news from Mrs Dalrymple, but her sister's brief friendship with Miranda had petered out.

After weeks of careful nursing, Mr Castle became as well as he was ever likely to be and it was improbable that he would ever be able to resume his full parochial duties. A semi-retirement seemed inevitable, with consequent fall in income. Charity knew she must find herself a job, and with no word from Carne after nearly three months, it seemed unlikely that she would still be needed as Frances' nannie. The post must have been filled.

Then one September morning, with a foretaste of autumn in the air, a letter arrived from Jason. Her heart gave a lurch at the sight of the firm black script. He called her, 'My dear Charity,' and asked how her father was getting along, going on to enquire if there was any chance of her return to Carne. They had tried a temporary governess for Frances with unsuccessful results. She would greatly relieve their domestic problems if she would come back. Except for the opening, it was a chill, formal note, and somehow disappointing, but what could she expect? A love letter? A declaration of friendship? She was only the ex-nannie, a last resort since her successor had failed. Though she had cherished the memory of the night when Jason had soothed and comforted her, she could not pretend that he had been motivated by anything stronger than the tender compassion he would have shown to Frances if the child had had a nightmare. He had never thought of her as an adult woman—had he not told her at Buxton she might have been Frances' sister? But Charity desperately wanted to see him again, and there were still several months before Frances' parents returned. She had done her duty by her father, and surely now she was entitled to return to Carne for a brief respite before she faced up to working in a children's home?

When she broached the subject to her mother, Mrs Castle wailed:

'I thought you'd come home for good!'

'You know you can't afford to keep me,' Charity pointed out. 'I'll have to get a job, and I might as well finish the one I had up north.'

Tearfully, Mrs Castle agreed, but Charity remembered that there was still Miranda to be considered, and it was significant that Jason had not mentioned his aunt, and Mrs Dalrymple had not written to support his plea. If she were still incensed against Charity for her repudiation of Gabriel, life at Carne would not be very pleasant, and she had no clue to Miranda's feelings. So she hesitated, wondering if she could broach the subject to Jason, and did not immediately answer his letter.

October had come in, a golden October with the trees turning to red and gold, and the brilliant blooms of late summer still decorating the flower beds, dahlias, chrysanthemums and Michaelmas daisies, for there had as yet been no frost, when Miranda rang up. Charity, who had answered the phone, nearly dropped the receiver when she heard the familiar cold voice.

'When are you coming back?' Mrs Dalrymple demanded imperiously. 'Didn't you get Jason's letter? That father of yours must be recovered by now, and

Frances is quite unbearable. She doesn't get enough exercise now Paula and Jason are engrossed in their show jumping exhibits, and Annie's given notice. I'm at my wits' end what to do with the child.'

'I'll come up tomorrow,' Charity said.

It was a long and tedious journey. Early mist delayed the local train and she missed her connection at Euston. The train she caught was dirty and slow, very different from the V.I.P. treatment she had received when she had come up to London. She travelled via Stafford and as the hills began to appear, she peered eagerly from the carriage window to view them. She wondered if Jason would come to meet her and her heart beat fast with eager anticipation as the train stopped at the station, but only Pat was there.

'Pleased to see you back, miss,' he greeted her.

'I'm glad to be back,' she said simply.

Throughout the drive up to the Clough, her anticipation increased. How would Jason greet her? Would he have reverted to his former cold formality? She thought that was hardly likely now, there had been too much between them; more probably he would extend to her the kind indulgence he would give to a child. Again she was disappointed. Mrs Dalrymple met her at the hall door, alone.

'Thank God you've come!' she said. 'Now I'll get some peace. Whatever possessed me to take charge of Martin's kid, I can't imagine—I must have been crazy.' Pat went by carrying Charity's cases. 'The same rooms, Pat,' she called to him. 'Come down when you're ready, Charity, since there's only the two of us we'll have supper together. Paula and Jason are in London, competing in the Horse of the Year Show. We'll be able to watch them on the television.'

So Jason was not at Carne, and Charity felt sick, as her eager anticipations faded. There was a scuffle overhead and a small figure came flying down the stairs to hurl itself into her arms.

'Oh, Nannie, Nannie, is you really come?'

Charity buried her face in the flaxen hair. Frances' welcome almost compensated for Jason's absence.

Up in the schoolroom Charity was introduced to an enormous doll which could walk and even talk when appropriate strings were pulled.

'Wherever did you get that?' she asked.

'Burfday present from Mummy and Daddy,' Frances said proudly. 'I'd lots and lots of toys, but it's ever so long ago.' She looked despondent, then cheered up to add, 'Now I'll look forward to Christmas.'

'Will you?' Charity laughed. 'What did you do on your birthday?'

'Uncle Jason and Paula took me to Castleton,' Frances informed her, and with a pang Charity remembered how Jason had planned that excursion before he knew of her own treachery with Gabriel. So Paula had gone in her stead, even though she was not fond of children. Perhaps she had been trying to ingratiate herself with Jason ... Charity chided herself for the unkind thought.

'We went into a big cave with stac ... stal ...' Frances stumbled over the word.

'Stalactites,' Charity prompted.

'That's it. They was all lit up and so pretty, and I gotted something for you.'

'For me? How sweet of you, darling, but you didn't know I'd come back.'

'You said you would, and Uncle Jason said you would,' the child insisted. She pulled at Charity's hand. 'Come on and see what I got.'

Charity went with her into her little room, marvelling that Jason had been so sure she would return. Frances opened a drawer from which she produced an object wrapped in tissue paper.

'There,' she said, 'isn't it nice?'

Unwrapping the paper, Charity found a little bowl made of the Blue John Spa that Jason had told her was only found in Derbyshire. The colour was more mauve than blue with darker veining, and it had been exquisitely shaped and polished. Charity held it in her hands suspecting that it had cost far more than the child's limited pocket money. So, even when she had been miles away, Jason had remembered he had promised her just such a souvenir.

'I told Uncle Jason to get you something,' Frances informed her, 'and he said to choose and I thought you'd like that. Do you?'

She looked at Charity expectantly.

'It's perfectly lovely, darling,' Charity told her. 'I shall treasure it always,' and not only because of Frances.

'He said it would be a mem ... mem ... I can't say it.'

'Memento? Yes, it will.'

A little piece of the Derbyshire hills to take away with her when she left Carne, in which to keep her cherished memories of Carne and Carne's owner. Perhaps he had meant it to be just that.

Charity settled the reluctant Frances in bed before she went to join Miranda for supper and television. She was eager to see Jason on the silver screen, it was next best to beholding him in the flesh, and he always looked superb on a horse. Having washed and tidied herself, she was whiling away the time before the gong went by putting the schoolroom to rights. It had suffered since Annie's departure, for her successor was a slipshod sixteen-year-old from the Clough, called Melanie, whose ideas about cleanliness and order were rudimentary. There was a pile of papers upon the work table that ought not to have been there, an accumulation of several weeks. Idly Charity skimmed through them before throwing them out. They represented Melanie's reading material, brought in to enliven the hours she had to spend with Frances. Mixed up with fashion papers and comics were several editions of the local weekly news. One of these was folded at the page announcing births, deaths, marriages and engagements, and against one paragraph was a large red cross. Charity read about Jason Ollenshaw's of

Carne Hall, Cheshire, engagement to Miss Paula Stella Stevens of Woodlands in the same county, 'a union,' the paragraph went on, 'between two well-known equestrian families, that will be hailed with delight in sporting circles.'

Charity stared at the paper as if she had seen a snake. Her anticipations regarding Jason's welcome had been vague, but she had not expected to find that he was contemplating matrimony. Dimly she had surmised that their friendship would continue from the point when she had parted with him, and the night of the storm was still vivid in her mind. Now he had erected a barrier between them and October had finally succumbed to the charms of May.

She turned the paper to look at the date and discovered that the engagement had been announced before he had written to her, but he had not mentioned it in his letter. No doubt he considered that his personal affairs were so far beyond her sphere that it would not occur to him to refer to it. The omission hurt her more than the notice did, it emphasised the distance between them that she had hoped had shortened. The master of Carne did not condescend to inform his dependants of his forthcoming marriage.

It was no concern of hers, for doubtless it would not take place until after Frances had gone to join her parents and she had left Carne, but after all he had said to her, she felt that Jason might have given her his confidence.

But preparations for the event would be beginning, and Charity began to wish fervently that she had not come back.

To watch Paula's possession of Jason would cause her pain, though she might have foreseen it. Miranda and Gabriel had talked of the possibility and throughout her stay at Carne, Paula had often been there, and frequently in Jason's company. Frances had told her he had taken Paula to Castleton with them in her stead. She had taken his assertions about never marrying in good faith, without realising how quickly a man might change his mind given sufficient inducement.

Paula was at Wembley with him now, and together they would share their triumphs, while she, poor fool, would have to sit and watch them on television, knowing that she was forever exiled from their world.

Now they were engaged, they would be absorbed in each other and their common pursuit. Miranda's phone message should have given her a clue, if she had not been so engrossed in her own fantasies. She had said they were devoting all their time to their show exhibits, implying that Frances was left out. She had been summoned to keep the child out of the way, and there would be no more rides with Jason on the moors.

Charity was tempted to send word to Miranda that she was too tired to come downstairs, but it would only be postponing the ordeal, which sooner or later must be faced. The Show went on all the week.

Besides, Miranda was alone and wanting company, even her company. She had said nothing about her nephew's engagement, but she probably thought Charity knew about it, or, more likely, that it would be of no interest to her.

Perhaps it would be easier to see Jason and Paula on the screen before she had to meet them in the flesh, and by so doing accustom herself to their togetherness.

She only hoped Miranda would not enlarge upon the subject that night. In the days to come she would have to steel herself to listening to wedding talk and plans, but at that moment, her wound was still raw, and she felt that she could not bear it.

That, however, she was spared, for Mrs Dalrymple made no reference to her nephew's engagement. She asked perfunctorily after Charity's family, and grumbled about the domestic staff at Carne. Mrs Appleton was getting past it, and Annie's replacement most unsatisfactory. Charity reflected that she would regard Jason's marriage no more favourably than she did. She had always feared that he would marry and Gabriel be dispossessed.

The television was on throughout the meal, which

was served in the morning room, dispensing with the need for further conversation, and it was not until it was finished that the show-jumping came on. Both Jason and Paula were competing in various events. Watching them, Charity had to admit that they were a well matched pair. Both were exquisitely turned out in well-fitting riding clothes, both supremely in command of the beautiful creatures they bestrode. In close-up she saw Jason's face, a little grim, a little taut, and she noticed how he patted his horse's neck after a good round, while his face broke into the charming smile that dispelled its harshness. Her heart ached. He was so very dear and so completely remote. Paula in contrast was all smiles whenever her face was visible. She looked superb and she knew it. She took her jumps with stylish confidence. Neither she nor Jason were faulted.

'The most important events are on Saturday night,' Miranda told her. 'I don't mind betting that Jason's Emperor is acclaimed the Horse of the Year.' In her cold way she became almost animated, and Charity recalled that she had been an Ollenshaw and been bred among horses.

'I've promised Frances she shall stay up for the last night,' Miranda went on. 'I'm delighted that at last she's become keen on riding.'

Which she probably would have been from the start if Gabriel had not intimidated her, Charity thought. She wondered what had happened to him, but she did not like to ask. However, as the evening wore on, Mrs Dalrymple became confidential. She was tired of her own company.

'Gabriel's taken up with a girl called Samantha Davis,' she said, with an oblique glance at Charity.

Startled, Charity exclaimed: 'The one he nearly crippled?'

'I suppose Jason told you that.' Miranda spoke stiffly. 'He exaggerates so. Samantha was involved in an accident, it's true, and for some reason she blamed Gabriel and broke off their engagement. Rather mean of her, I think.'

So that was Miranda's version, Charity thought wryly.

'Well, now it seems they've met again,' Miranda went on. 'They've made up their differences and are to be married quite soon. Then they're off to Spain.'

She glanced at Charity maliciously as she gave this news and Charity did feel a slight pang, but less for Gabriel's defection than for the bursting of a fairy bubble. Once Spain and Gabriel had seemed the epitome of romance, until she had discovered the dark depths in Gabriel's character.

'I hope they'll be very happy,' she said sincerely.

'I'm sure they will be. Samantha seems quite besotted with him now. About time someone appreciated my boy. Put another log on, please, Charity, this place is already beginning to feel like an ice-house. Thank goodness this'll be my last winter here. I'm going to live with a friend in the South of France.'

When Jason is married, Charity thought, looking sadly round the familiar room, which Paula would no doubt redecorate. Both the man to whom she had nearly become engaged and the man she loved were getting married and her job at a children's home, which represented her own future, seemed dreary.

Miranda remarked that it was getting late and Charity must be tired, and they parted amicably for the night.

Next morning, at Miranda's insistence, she renewed her acquaintance with Lola and she and Frances set out for their morning ride. The ling was still out and the moors were clothed in royal purple with here and there a patch of golden gorse, but her pleasure was marred, for it was the season of grouse shooting, and the moors they had previously traversed were out of bounds. Apart from the restriction, Charity did not like to think of the slaughter of the shy birds, and she did not enjoy the roast grouse she was presented with for dinner, but Miranda laughed and said men must have their sport and the letting of the grouse moors was a valuable source of income.

'Jason doesn't care much for game shooting,' she said contemptuously, 'so he lets the shooting.'

Charity was glad to hear that.

On their second morning, Frances suggested riding over towards Woodlands, and Charity, who had not seen Macclesfield Forest, agreed. She was curious to see Paula's home, though she had no wish to encounter the Stevens family, but they need not do that if they kept on the road. However, she had reckoned without Frances. They turned off the Clough road to take a winding lane over a shoulder of green hill. On the further side, they were among trees, serried masses of young conifers, the work of the Forestry Commission. The road began to descend through older beeches, finally reaching a cleared space in a valley bottom. Here they came upon an old grey farmhouse set among green paddocks; further along in the distance was the glint of water, shining through the tree trunks, where the reservoir had been built.

'What a pretty spot!' Charity exclaimed, drawing rein to look about her.

'If we go and knock at the door, Aunt Mary might give me a drink,' Frances said insinuatingly. 'I's ever so thirsty.'

Not wishing to meet Jason's future in-laws, Charity said hastily that they must not bother Mrs Stevens, but at that moment a man came out of the farm yard, waving his hand to them.

'Uncle Joe!' Frances screamed.

The man who approached them reminded Charity of Jason, the same lean, spruce figure, the same long brown face, but he was shorter and his eyes were dark.

'Hullo, brat,' he exclaimed cheerfully, 'come to pay us a visit, have you?' He looked at Charity doubtfully.

'My nannie,' Frances explained.

'Yes, of course, Miss Castle, isn't it? My daughter has spoken about you—come in, won't you?'

'I don't think we've time, thank you ...' she was beginning, but he cut her short.

'Nonsense, my wife would never forgive me if I let you go away without some refreshment.'

'And I's so thirsty,' Frances reiterated.

'There you are,' Joe Stevens exclaimed triumphantly, 'we must do something about the child's thirst.'

Charity knew by now the north-countryman's boundless hospitality, and that if she once entered the house, she could not escape without being fed, but in the face of Frances' determination, she had no choice. Joe took the horses and told Frances to take her into the kitchen where his wife was cooking. It was a vast, low-ceilinged room, its stone-paved floor covered with rag mats. A big, old-fashioned kitchen range, polished to shine like silver, gave a cheerful glow, though there was an electric cooker in one corner. Mary Stevens greeted them warmly and turned a huge tabby cat off the one easy chair so that Charity could sit in it. Along one wall was a fine carved settle, the hardness of its wooden seat mitigated by cushions upon which Frances perched herself. Having supplied the child with a tumbler of milk and pressed upon Charity a glass of her plum wine, which Charity took a little dubiously, Mary asked if she would try a piece of her parkin.

'Real old-fashioned stuff,' she said proudly. 'That and oatcake was what you'd find in every Derbyshire home, but now it's all mass-produced rubbish from the shops. Nobody does their own baking. I still make my own bread,' she pointed to a basin full of dough that had been put in front of the fire to rise, 'and that's made of wheat, not potatoes.'

Charity accepted a slice of parkin, a dark sort of gingerbread, aware of a slight bewilderment. Paula's family were not in the least what she had expected. They seemed a homely couple and she had thought they would be starchy County, but they were obviously prosperous and their homestead was their own property, assets which had made Paula acceptable in Jason's eyes, for one day Woodlands would be hers, as she was an only child. She told Mrs Stevens that she had been watching the show jumping, and Mrs Stevens' eyes shone with pride. She was a comely woman, with her daughter's dark colouring, and obviously her daughter meant everything to her.

'Paula's a fine horsewoman,' she declared, 'God bless her! And she's a good girl, too, Miss Castle, she doesn't let her successes go to her head. She's going to make her man a good wife. True, she's not over-fond of baking, but she can cook all those French fancy dishes you see pictures of in the magazines, not that she'll need to do much cooking up at the Hall, and she can sew too. She's making her own wedding dress—haute couture's got nothing on her. Would you like to see it? She wouldn't mind if I showed it to you. Of course it isn't finished, it's all hand-embroidered and that takes a lot of time. Paula's a dab hand at embroidery, and she looks pretty as a picture when she's working on it with her head full of dreams.'

Charity flinched away from the image thus conjured up of the lovesick Paula stitching at her wedding gown, and since she was making it, the event must be nearer than she had thought, but she shrank from seeing the garment in which Paula would give herself to Jason, and at risk of wounding the mother's beaming pride, she said hastily:

'I'd rather wait to see it when it's finished. It'll spoil the effect to see it half done, and Frances and I ought to be going, or we'll be late for lunch.'

She put down the cat which had sprung upon her knees and called to Frances, who came reluctantly. Evidently she found Woodlands congenial and had dug herself into the Stevens' affections when she had stayed there.

The Stevens saw them off with invitations to come again, and waved to them as they rode away. They trotted up through the woods back into the stone-wall country and the green slopes of the hills, while Frances chattered gaily about Uncle Joe and Aunt Mary.

'They said I must go and stay with them when Paula

is married,' she said blithely, 'as they won't have any little girl any more.'

There was no escaping the impact of the coming marriage, and again Charity wished that she had not returned to Carne. She had so far been able to ignore it, principally because Miranda never mentioned Jason's nuptials, the subject no doubt being a sore one with her. The nearest she got to it was while they were listening to the applause Paula had won after completing a faultless round.

'She'll miss all that excitement when she's married,' Miranda remarked icily.

'But she needn't give it up, need she?' Charity asked.

'Perhaps not at first, but when the babies start coming, it won't be so easy.'

Charity felt a fresh stab. Jason had changed his mind about the offspring who might prefer machines to horses.

On the other hand, Mrs Dalrymple talked freely about Gabriel and Samantha, with many a sly glance at Charity as if she hoped she would betray regret. Apparently she was in touch with Miss Davis, who seemed to be fonder of her than her son was.

Charity thought a great deal about the other girl, who was, she gathered, several years older than herself and much more sophisticated. Miranda emphasised her devotion to Gabriel, and she must have conquered the doubts which had caused her to try to break her engagement with such disastrous consequences. Perhaps if she loved him so much, she might be able to influence him and check his failings.

Frances, as promised, was allowed to stay up on the Saturday night to watch the final events. Paula, competing for the Ladies' Cup, won with ease, and Emperor, as Miranda had foretold, was designated Horse of the Year.

The winners were lined up to receive their awards from royalty, and Jason looked proud and a little arrogant as he sat upon his equally proud horse. Charity's heart yearned towards him.

178

'Is that really Uncle Jason?' Frances asked, awe-struck.

'Of course it is, you silly child,' Miranda exclaimed impatiently. 'Who else do you think it is?'

'He looks like a prince,' Frances sighed.

'Don't be ridiculous,' her fond grandmother snapped. 'You won't find anything very prince-like about him when he comes home tomorrow. He's sure to be very bad-tempered after all the strain and excitement, so you'd better keep out of his way.'

'He's never cross with me like you is,' Frances said candidly.

'Go to bed,' Miranda told her, 'and don't be rude.'

Charity took the child's hand and bade her say good-night. Together they walked up the stairs to bed. To-morrow Jason would be home.

Actually he did not arrive until the following day. He rang up Miranda to tell her he would be back by dinner time, but he was going to Woodlands first to escort Paula. Charity, who was passing through the hall on her way to the stables, heard Miranda say:

'Why don't you bring Paula over for dinner?'

Jason's reply was of course inaudible, but Mrs Dalrymple laughed and exclaimed, 'Oh, love's young dream!'

Charity gritted her teeth, and ran out into the October sunshine. There would be no end to the pinpricks she would have to bear when Jason returned.

The next day dawned, and she learned she was to be banished to the schoolroom for her evening meal. Miranda had suddenly remembered that it had been the master's orders that the nannie should dine upstairs.

'So I'm afraid it's the end of our cosy little suppers in the morning room,' she told Charity regretfully. 'Jason likes the chilly state of the dining room, and of course it's his house, so his wishes are paramount.'

Charity, who knew that the reason for her isolation had been Gabriel's presence, tried not to feel hurt, reflecting that since Paula was going to dine with the family, she would prefer to stay upstairs. Frances, too, in spite of her pleas, was sent to bed early. Miranda, Paula and Jason wanted a clear field to leaven their meal with an inquest upon all the show-jumping performances, a proceeding in which Charity and Frances would have no part, as yet, for Frances said, as Charity bade her goodnight:

'When I's a big girl, I'm going to jump and win *all* the prizes.'

'Perhaps you will,' Charity agreed. 'One never knows.'

When Frances was a big girl, where would she herself be? At best the warden of a children's home, with Carne and Jason a dim memory. Fiercely she told herself, she could never forget Jason Ollenshaw, and she did not want to forget him.

> ''Tis change that paineth and the bitterness
> Of life's decay when joy has ceased to be
> That makes dark all the earth.'

Joy would have ceased to be and the earth would be very dark when the time came for her to leave Carne.

CHAPTER NINE

With Frances in bed and asleep, Charity sat in the schoolroom with a basket of mending—Frances was forever tearing her clothes—and tried not to listen for the sounds of arrival below. The light was dying behind Shuttlings Low, and she sternly repressed an urge to stand at the window to watch for the expected car. Not that she would see it, the view from the window did not extend to the front of the house, but she would see the light from the headlamps, and if she opened the sash, she might hear his voice. But Melanie would be bringing up her dinner and Charity did not want to be caught by the maid hanging out of the window to glimpse the master's return.

Melanie had all the modern teenager's contempt for her betters. She thought the régime at Carne was old hat and Charity a fool to work there. She herself only intended to stay until some better opening presented itself. Sure enough, she arrived with her tray, letting the door swing to behind her, but not before Charity caught the distant murmur of voices from the hall. So Jason and Paula had arrived.

'The big noise is back,' Melanie said in confirmation, banging the tray down on the small table beside Charity. 'Dinner in the dining room and Ma Appleton carrying on as if he were royalty.' She sniffed. 'He ain't no better than other folk.'

Charity said nothing. Useless to rebuke Melanie for lack of respect, she did not know the meaning of the word.

'You might bring your tray down when you've done,' Melanie suggested. 'I'm being run off my feet.'

'Certainly,' Charity said pleasantly, though she knew Annie would never have allowed her to do such a thing. Melanie departed with a flounce of her mini-skirt, which looked odd under her long apron, for she had been too lazy to shorten the latter, and a bang of the door. Charity picked at the food which was unappetising being half cold, and she had no appetite. She heard the dull boom of the dinner gong, and pictured the trio round the big polished table, Miranda cold and austere in velvet and lace, Paula in some exciting creation and Jason ... she sighed, she must not think of Jason, but she longed desperately to see his face, and there seemed no chance of that until tomorrow morning. She walked to the window, and drew the curtains. A full moon was rising behind the house and silvered the lawn which sparkled with a touch of frost, as if it were strewn with diamonds. Jason was under the same roof as she was, but he was as remote as the moon. She turned back, without drawing the curtains, picked up her tray and made for the back stairs. Mrs Appleton was in the kitchen and raised her brows as she appeared with her burden.

'T'lazy slut should have done that,' she objected.

'It was no trouble,' Charity told her, and went through into the hall. She lingered there, hoping to hear Jason's voice, but there was no sound, from behind the closed doors, either of voices or laughter. She was completely cut off from him. She went slowly upstairs, dreading the lonely evening in her own rooms, and ran straight into Jason in the passage. He had changed for the evening into a dark suit and white shirt, apparel in which she had never seen him before. It made him look taller and fairer and very distinguished. With his aquiline nose and sleek grooming Jason could not be mistaken for other than he was, the descendant of a long line of high-bred gentlemen.

'Charity!' he exclaimed, smiling with evident pleasure. 'I was beginning to wonder what had happened to you. My aunt told me that you'd come back, of course, but why weren't you at dinner?'

'Because I seem to remember it was you who insisted that I should stay upstairs,' she said demurely, while her heart beat so fast it threatened to choke her.

'Did I? But that was a long time ago, before ...

where are you off to now?' as she moved away from him.

'Back to the schoolroom,' she said a little bitterly.

He stood aside to let her pass, but when she reached the door, she discovered that he was following her. He came in after her and closed the door, looking about him appreciatively.

'This is one of the most cosy rooms in the house,' he said. 'When Frances leaves us, we might use it as a sitting room.' He crossed to the window and looked out at the moon-flecked lawn. 'It has a nice look-out too.'

So he was planning how to arrange the house to receive his bride. Charity fiddled with her work basket while her heart swelled. The schoolroom had been her sanctum, now it was to be Paula's sitting room. He turned round from the window to look at her, the light shone on her bent brown head. She was wearing her little dark frock with the white collar and cuffs, and she looked very young and a little forlorn.

'What's the matter, Charity?' he asked.

She looked up quickly. 'Nothing. I was remembering I must congratulate you on your success. We watched it all on television. You must feel very proud of Emperor. He's a beautiful horse, isn't he?' There was a brittle quality in her voice, as memories from their last meeting in that room swept over her, but she must not show any emotion.

'Yes, Emperor's a fine beast,' he said absently.

He came to stand in front of her, and putting his fingers under her chin, he raised her face, but she kept her eyes resolutely downcast.

'Look at me,' he commanded.

Slowly she raised her heavy lashes, and her eyes, grey and clear as mountain pools, met his in a long look. Again she saw in the blue depths of his a flicker of flame. He dropped his hand with a sigh, and turned away from her.

'Oh, Charity, if only you weren't so young!'

'That's a fault that will remedy with time,' she said

183

tartly. 'We grow old all too quickly.'

'We do,' he agreed, 'and I'll be old long before you will.'

'It doesn't follow,' she observed, wondering where all this was tending, 'women age more quickly than men, I think. Some become old frumps at forty, while I've met some spry young gentlemen of fifty. It all depends upon whether you let yourself age.' She thought he must be thinking of the gap in years between himself and Paula, for Miss Stevens was only two years older than herself, and she wanted to reassure him.

He laughed. 'Where did you gain so much knowledge?'

'Among my father's parishioners—there were all sorts at our village do's.'

'Yes, you're used to village life, you don't yearn for shops and bright lights?' he asked. 'You like Carne? You don't find it too isolated?'

'I love Carne,' she said simply.

His face brightened. 'Would you like to live here ... always?'

'Could I?' She remembered that domestic staff was always a problem at Carne. 'I mean, could you find a place for me here when Frances has gone?'

His eyes were crinkled with suppressed laughter, as he said:

'I think I might be able to do that.'

'And Miss Stevens wouldn't mind?'

'Paula?' he raised his brows questioningly.

'Yes, she'll be mistress here later on.'

'Uncle Jas!'

A small figure in a long nightgown was standing in the doorway leading into the bedroom. Charity never wholly closed the communicating doors when the child was in bed, knowing that Frances was subject to nervous fears.

'Fran, you naughty girl, you should be asleep,' Jason exclaimed.

'I wanted to stay up to see you, but Gran wouldn't let

184

me,' Frances explained, 'I waked up and heard voices and I knowed it was you.' She ran across the room and embraced Jason's leg. 'Has you brought me anything?' she demanded.

He stooped and picked her up. 'Yes, but you must wait until the morning for it. It's too late now.'

Frances pouted. 'What is it?'

'You'll have to wait and see. Was it I or the present that you wanted to see?'

Frances, young as she was, was not without diplomacy when dealing with men. 'You, Uncle,' she said, nuzzling in Jason's neck, from whence her voice came muffled. 'Has you brought Nannie anything?'

'Yes,' Jason affirmed, 'but whether she'll accept it or not, I don't know.' He looked at Charity quizzically over the child's head.

'Mr Ollenshaw, you shouldn't ...' Charity began, her face flushing.

'Wait and see what it is,' he cut in. 'Perhaps you're right, and I shouldn't, that'll be for you to judge. Come on, Fran, it's time you were asleep, or you won't be fresh for your ride in the morning.'

'Uncle Jas,' Frances lifted a sleepy head, 'can I be Paula's bridesmaid? Aunt Mary says I's too little, but she'd ask you. You will say yes, won't you?'

'I think that's a matter for Paula to decide,' he returned. He walked through to Frances' room, carrying the child, but Charity did not follow them. His words recalled the immediacy of his marriage, which she had forgotten in the first joy of seeing him again. She had been crazy to suggest staying at Carne to wait upon Paula. That would require a self-immolation too great to bear. She heard smothered giggles from Frances' room, and then Jason came back, closing the intervening bedroom door firmly behind him.

'Too bad that Martin has had to miss a whole year of Fran's childhood,' he said. 'She's at an enchanting age, and they grow up so quickly.'

'Was it impossible for them to have her with them?' she asked, aware that he was looking at her intently.

'No, but not wise. They're in Africa, organising a new branch out there, and there are all sorts of risks.' He sighed. 'Martin has to put his business first. Do sit down, Charity, you look so aloof standing up there.'

She obeyed, sinking into her low chair, and he took another on the opposite side of the hearth in which a small fire burnt brightly.

'Certainly a woman's presence makes a room feel like home,' he said contentedly. 'If only I had my pipe.'

'Don't you always carry it?'

'Not in these clothes.' He looked at her enigmatically. 'They were put on for an occasion.'

'Ah yes,' she said, with a pang, 'and shouldn't you be downstairs? Miss Stevens will be wondering where you are.'

'Paula couldn't come tonight, she had another and more important date—and that reminds me, what did you mean when you said she'd be mistress here?'

'But you'll live here, won't you, after you're married?'

'I couldn't live anywhere else, that's what I've been trying to tell you. Good God!' he sprang to his feet. 'Did you by any chance see that notice in the local paper?'

'Yes, I did. I ... I found it here, on the table.'

'How the deuce did it get there?' he demanded. 'But no matter. It was an error, Charity. Paula is going to be married, but not to me. She's engaged to a certain James Openshaw of Bowden Hall at Fernilee. I suppose as she's so often ridden with me, and the initials are the same, the local reporter got us muddled up. Of course the announcement was corrected, but you didn't see that?'

She shook her head. 'No, and everything pointed to you and Paula ... I thought you ... loved her?' She could not quite believe what he had told her. Paula and Jason had been linked together in her mind for so long.

'Actually I believe she did once have a bit of a

186

schoolgirl crush on me,' he said, quite without complacency, 'but I discouraged it. I had to be cruel to be kind, and no one is more pleased than I am that she has got herself engaged to someone else.'

The joy that Charity had felt at his revelation was suddenly quenched. How hard he was, and invulnerable! He could deliberately snub Paula's girlish passion for him on the plea of being cruel to be kind. How much more cruel would he be to herself if he ever suspected her own folly? She turned her eyes, which she had raised to his face full of eager hope, back to the fire and her lips drooped.

'Didn't you realise that you might have broken her heart?' she asked reproachfully.

'There was no question of that, Charity,' he said earnestly. 'She only had a crush on me because we were thrown so much together. James suits her a lot better than I would, and he spends half the year in London. I've no use for the swinging capital, but Paula ... swings!' he smiled. 'She and James were celebrating her success well into the small hours while I was longing for home. Events have proved how wise I was not to become involved with her.'

'Oh yes, you're very wise,' Charity cried bitterly, 'so calculating and cold. I don't believe you're capable of loving any woman.' Against her will a note of despair crept into her voice.

He looked at her in surprise. 'But don't you know ...' he began.

'Yes, I know.' She sprang to her feet to face him, her eyes ablaze, all the pent-up emotion of the past few days welling up in her and overflowing in passionate storm.. 'You'd never make the mistake I did over Gabriel, you haven't enough heart. You've never married because you've never found a woman who was the right age, the right class and had the right qualities. Paula was too young and giddy, I'm too young and childish,' she had become reckless, 'but we've got hearts that can feel, while you ... you're an iceberg ...'

187

She was stopped in mid-tirade, for in one swift movement he had pulled her into his arms and his mouth silenced her.

It seemed a long time afterwards before she emerged from the rapturous ecstasy that had swept away all coherent thought. She was sitting on Jason's knees, her hair in wild disorder about her face, her arms still draped about his neck, while his firmly clasped her waist.

'Do you still think I'm an iceberg?' he murmured in her ear.

'More like a volcano,' she whispered back, hiding her flushed face in his neck.

'I'll tell you now what I've brought you,' he went on. 'It's my mother's ring. I've had it cleaned and I hope it will fit you. So if you can bring yourself to marry a crusty old bachelor, who has only now found the right woman, I'm yours, and so is Carne.'

She did not answer him in words, but presently she slid from his arms and sat at his feet, with her head against his knees, while he played with her long hair.

'When did you first begin to think of me as human,' she asked mischievously, 'and not merely as Frances' nannie?'

'When you shaped so well on a horse, of course,' he returned, smiling. 'But I found you very appealing at our first meeting. That's why I was so loath to expose you to Gabriel's wiles, and when you had that fall and thought I was my cousin——' His face darkened. 'I'm ashamed to confess it, but I was wildly jealous.'

'Is that why you were so cold and severe afterwards? You were, you know.'

'Yes. I should have known better at my age. I hoped to frighten you into keeping away from Gabriel, with no success, naturally, but I couldn't bear to think of you throwing yourself away upon that young ruffian. You would be quite incapable of taming him and once the novelty had worn off, he would have deserted you.'

'I daresay, but if only you'd told me why he wanted

to get married . . .'

'It wouldn't have made any difference if you were really infatuated, and I feared you were. You would only have thought I was trying to put you against him, and I should have rattled the family skeleton for nothing. As it was, when I did tell you, you were still half bewitched by him.'

'Bewitched is the right word, he had me spellbound —he was so very good-looking.'

'I'm afraid I can't compete with him for looks . . .' Jason said ruefully. 'I'm a leathery old horseman.'

'Darling, I love your face, and it isn't looks that count. I believe that in my heart I always knew I loved you, and I never really cared for him.'

'Well, you hid it very well. It was only on the night of the thunderstorm that I began to hope. You said Carne was a lovely place, but you immediately had to qualify your praise by saying you might get fed up with it in time.'

'I said that because I was afraid you might suspect how much I wanted to live here always—with you.'

'Why shouldn't I suspect? If I had I wouldn't have let you go, or at any rate I would have come with you. Oh, Charity, the house seemed so dreary and empty while you've been gone. In the end I couldn't bear it any longer. I had to try to get you back.'

'Well, I came . . .'

'And I'll never let you leave me again.'

'I don't want to—ever—and Jason . . .' She hid her face against his knee.

'Well, darling, what is it?'

'You won't mind having a son, will you? Even if he does prefer motor-bikes.'

He laughed. 'We'll have to take that risk, but it might be a daughter—even daughters——'

'Daddy had three.'

'Faith, Hope and Charity, and the greatest of these is Charity—which should be translated as love.'

He drew her up into his arms again, while outside the moon clothed the moorland slopes with silver and inside the thick walls of the old house, silence brooded and the shadows gathered in the corners. They were no longer menacing, they represented home and the promise of deep content.

have you heard about Harlequin's great new series?

Harlequin Presents

* ANNE HAMPSON
* ANNE MATHER
* VIOLET WINSPEAR

These three very popular Harlequin authors have written many outstanding romances which we have not been able to include in the regular Harlequin series.

Now we have made special arrangements to publish many of these delightful never — before — available stories in a new author series, called "Harlequin Presents".

See reverse of page for complete listing of titles available.

Harlequin Presents..

Three of the world's greatest romance authors.
Don't miss any of this new series. Only 75c each!

ANNE HAMPSON

- [ ] #1 GATES OF STEEL
- [ ] #2 MASTER OF MOONROCK
- [ ] #7 DEAR STRANGER
- [ ] #10 WAVES OF FIRE
- [ ] #13 A KISS FROM SATAN

- [ ] #16 WINGS OF NIGHT
- [ ] #19 SOUTH OF MANDRAKI
- [ ] #22 THE HAWK AND THE DOVE
- [ ] #25 BY FOUNTAINS WILD
- [ ] #28 DARK AVENGER

ANNE MATHER

- [ ] #3 SWEET REVENGE
- [ ] #4 THE PLEASURE & THE PAIN
- [ ] #8 THE SANCHEZ TRADITION
- [ ] #11 WHO RIDES THE TIGER
- [ ] #14 STORM IN A RAIN BARREL
- [ ] #17 LIVING WITH ADAM

- [ ] #20 A DISTANT SOUND OF THUNDER
- [ ] #23 THE LEGEND OF LEXANDROS
- [ ] #26 DARK ENEMY
- [ ] #29 MONKSHOOD

VIOLET WINSPEAR

- [ ] #5 DEVIL IN A SILVER ROOM
- [ ] #6 THE HONEY IS BITTER
- [ ] #9 WIFE WITHOUT KISSES
- [ ] #12 DRAGON BAY
- [ ] #15 THE LITTLE NOBODY

- [ ] #18 THE KISSES AND THE WINE
- [ ] #21 THE UNWILLING BRIDE
- [ ] #24 PILGRIM'S CASTLE
- [ ] #27 HOUSE OF STRANGERS
- [ ] #30 BRIDE OF LUCIFER

To: HARLEQUIN READER SERVICE, Dept. N 312

M.P.O. Box 707, Niagara Falls, N.Y. 14302

Canadian address: Stratford, Ont., Canada

- [ ] Please send me the free Harlequin Romance Presents Catalogue.

- [ ] Please send me the titles checked.

I enclose $_____ (No C.O.D.'s). All books are 75c each. To help defray postage and handling cost, please add 25c.

Name _____

Address _____

City/Town _____

State/Prov. _____ Zip _____

N 312